# BLACK

# KNIGHT

# APOCALYPSE

THE

DISINTEGRATION

TRILOGY

BOOK

ONE


THE

ARIMATHEAN

SAGA

BOOK

THREE

A NOVEL

BY

# SEAN
# LEARY

ISBN # (eBook) tba

ISBN # (Print book)  978-0692618417

Library of Congress Catalog Card Number: Applied for

First edition eBook: 12/19/2016

First edition print: 12/12/2016

Cover and interior design by Sean Leary.

Website: www.seanleary.com. Email:
seanleary@seanleary.com.


Very special thanks, as always, to my son, Jackson.
Everything I do, I dedicate to you, my best friend and
beautiful boy. I love you.


Very special thanks as well to Matthew and Pam Clemens,
for your incredible support, advice, and friendship.


Thanks as well to Sara Holtz, Jess Rueve, Ross Parse, Tim
Novotny, Donna Pesavento, Frances Iskalis, Jan Larsen, Bill
Wimbiscus, Erik Larsen, Terry Kissinger, Joni Abbott,
Tristan Tapscott, Linda Cook, Bill and Gail Leary, Mary and
David Stacel, Dan O'Shea and Johanna Harris, and all of my
family, friends, fans and readers everywhere, particularly my
readers and friends on Facebook.

As Always,

**FOR**

**JACKSON**

# What Critics And Fans Are Saying About 'The Arimathean' Saga...

"What an incredibly imaginative book! A terrific and original concept!"

 *--- Diana Gabaldon*

 *Author of The Outlander series*


"This book rocks. That pretty much says it all. It just rocks. It really is a non-stop, action-packed popcorn book where the fun never ends. I enjoyed reading it immensely. I'm really looking forward to the sequels."

 *--- Matthew Clemens*

 *Best-selling author, "No One Will Hear You."*


"Lovely imagery... very nice descriptive turns of phrase and a great, action-packed plot. There doesn't' seem to be an end to Sean Leary's imagination. The way he combines so many different genres and elements is incredibly entertaining."

 *--- Connie Corcoran Wilson*

 *Best-selling author, "Hellfire and Damnation"*

"A real surprise, in a great way... a non-stop thrill ride of action! Full of huge thrills and stunning twists, smart writing, and surprising heart. A book that will please action fans and fans of Christian fantasy alike, while pandering to neither. And in the end, a book of endless entertainment that makes you think, about life, about faith and about what drives us. A must-read."

*--- Alison Baker*

*Yahoo! News Chicago*

"Wow! Sean Leary is the new Stephen King."

*--- Geeta Razack*

*The Geeta Razack Blog*

"Imaginative and moving... a powerful work."

*--- Father John Comerford*

*Joliet Catholic Academy*

"It takes a lively and inventive writer to cast the three wise men as ninja wizards. It takes a great writer to enrich and deepen such a high concept notion and create an exciting and compelling story as Sean Leary has done with 'The Arimathean.'"

*--- Sean Patrick*

*Morning show host, WOC-AM*


"At first, when Sean Leary described his new novel `The Arimathean,' I thought he had lost it. Ninjas and the Nativity – seriously? But he tells it here with seriousness and, above all, respect, with dialogue that fleshes out his characters and solid action that keeps the reader turning the pages. And don't skip to the last pages or you'll cheat yourself out of a finale that's truly grand."

*--- Linda Cook*

*Award-winning critic / Iowa Press Women*

"A bloody, gory, fight-filled adventure story...
but here's the thing: this book is UPLIFTING. Gross at
times, yes, intense throughout. But it also has that feel
good quality a good adventure story must have.
Whether you take that as a "Glory of God" message or
just a "it feels awesome to kick evil's ass" message is up
to you. The book puts no pressure on you to choose.
Just enjoy the ride whatever way you want."

*--- **William Pepper***

***The William Pepper Blog***


"Black Knight Apocalypse is a smart, cool and very,
very entertaining ride! It's 'Ancient Aliens' crossed with
'The Matrix' and Leary's pulse-pounding, propulsive,
unique style of writing. Pulling together some of the
best-known and most entertaining conspiracy theories
into one thrilling, brilliant and most importantly, fun,
book is a tall order, but Leary has done it in a huge
way. Highly recommended!"

*--- **QuadCities.com***

"An incredibly cool concept – ninja wizards for the win! – and an even more awesome book. It's not just an amazing idea that Sean Leary's got here, it's a rockin' adventure story with a ton of action, but a surprising amount of heart. It'll thrill you with its imagination and cliffhangers, throw you a ton of curves and leave you wondering what's going to happen next and then out of the blue make you really think about these people and feel for what they're going through. A masterfully written book."

--- *Alternate Waves Comix Zine*

"Full of surprises and fast-paced action, both The Arimathean and The Blood of Destiny are amazing books. Highly recommended!"

--- *Adam Ripley*

*Nerdventures Blog*

# INTRODUCTION

I've always loved conspiracy theories.

But there's really no conspiracy when it comes to how the Arimathean saga has gone from a trilogy to a five-book (and possibly more) series.

When I first began writing the Arimathean saga, it was conceived as a trilogy.

The first book, The Arimathean, was about the Magi as ninja wizards, sent to protect Joseph and Mary from being killed by Satan (later called Satanus) and King Herod who were attempting to destroy them before they got to Bethlehem and Jesus was born. It was based on my Catholic upbringing and my love of such authors as J.R.R. Tolkien, C.S. Lewis, Michael Moorcock and others. As many critics and fans aptly put it, it was the Bible crossed with the Lord of the Rings. It meant all due respect to both, keeping the moral core of the source material while also adding a modern, action-packed spin.

In the second book, The Blood of Destiny, Satan is back again, with the Roman Emperor Tiberius, and they're trying to steal Jesus' body post-crucifixion/pre-resurrection so they can turn it into a zombie anti-Christ and take over the earth. The Magi are back, along with the 12 disciples, to battle various demons and prevent that from happening. The Blood of Destiny sets up the remainder of the trilogy, revealing that the Arimathean has become immortal and that he and Magdalene eventually go on to begin the Merovingian bloodline and the various secret societies within the world.

The third book, originally titled DisIntegration, was going to be all about the Book of Revelation and the end of the world. That's why the second book ends with John the Revelator landing on Patmos to write that book. It was originally going to be a modern take on Revelation, using current technology and science to describe the visions and prophecy of that book of the Bible. For example, the mark of the beast was the implanting of computer chips in people, etc.

But along the way, as I was doing tons of research for DisIntegration, I realized I had a lot of different stories I wanted to weave together, a lot of different details and characters, and they weren't going to fit into one book, unless that one book was massive.

Hence me deciding to change the Arimathean trilogy to the Arimathean saga, with five books planned, although leaving the door open to more.

Black Knight Apocalypse, the third book, is a bit of a reboot, or a new beginning, to the saga. While it contains a number of the characters from the first two books, it predominantly features new characters, it's predominantly set in 2042, and it jumps back and forth in time, going from 95 AD to

2042 and a lot of places in between. (Why 2042? I needed a future date, and it's an homage to Douglas Adams.) Interwoven into the story are a plethora of some of the best-known conspiracy theories spun over the past several centuries, everything from the Kennedy assassination to the Knights Templar to the moon landing to ancient aliens to the beginnings of various secret societies and more. It's easily been the most time consuming and elaborate novel, and book, I've ever written, given all the research. But it's also been an incredible ride and has involved an amazing amount of fascinating research into ancient cultures, religions, and heroic figures as well as various modern technologies and harbingers of the future. For everything that's in here, there's been an astounding amount of research that didn't get in. But I hope it's reflected in a positive way.

I think everyone loves conspiracy theories, and to the extent that's true, I hope a lot of you enjoy Black Knight Apocalypse, and the upcoming books in the Arimathean saga. They're all about fun, action-packed, propulsive science-fiction, and fantasy – the kinds of books I loved to read as a kid, and the kinds of books I still love to read. And I hope you do too.

As always, enjoy the trip . . .

Best wishes,

Sean Leary

# BLACK

# KNIGHT

# APOCALYPSE

# PRELUDE

**Berlin**

**April, 1945**

The blood moon curved in a jagged fang above them, a crimson slash across the velvet void engulfing them just before midnight.

They traveled on foot through the cold, across the thick trail of dead strewn upon the torn ground of the battlefield left behind.

They were two.

One, the man whose occult intelligence, cunning and connections within the clandestine pathways of this ravaged country had led them to this point. He was slight of build and clean-shaven, with the uniform of the enemy wrapped around him as a cloak of subterfuge. A daring blade of a man, wiry and clever, with a sleek black mane pulled back on his forehead above a sharp nose and cheekbones, and airy, pale green eyes floating alert and ethereal above a slice of a scar down the left side of his face.

He went by many names, held many passports to alight the paths for the secret organization he represented, the ancient sect of the Silent Hand. But he was born of a noble bloodline and named after the grandfather who had grown legendary in service of the same occult agency.

Dorin Xerxes.

The other man was the only one who could accompany him to fulfill their mission.

A dark, turbulent storm of being, armored in muscle and haloed in power and resonance, with a face of worn stone and eyes the color of charred earth at dawn, cut with an otherworldly gold.

He also held high rank in the Silent Hand, but within an ancient inner circle that even one as accomplished as Xerxes stood outside.

He was spoken of in hushed tones within their order, as the Fire of God, the One Who Could Not Die, the one who had lived for more than two millennia, who walked the earth as guardian until the next coming of the Christ.

Some said he was born Josephus, a man, once. Once.

But all called him by one name.

The Arimathean.

"We are close," the Arimathean said.

"You are sure?" Xerxes said.

The Arimathean glared at him, then stared ahead and continued, saying nothing.

"I am sorry, I know…" Xerxes said.

The Arimathean shook his head. "No need," he said.

"This has taken so long, much longer than we thought," Xerxes said. "There have been too many killed, too many sacrificed."

The Arimathean was silent, and Xerxes took note as the older man grew dark and brooding, and he remained silent as well.

The killing fields they strode across were ripe with death, and the Arimathean's mind flashed back to the camps.

They had freed many.

But not all.

And he remembered.

The one.

Her.

The woman in the camp. Her skin pale. Her lips pink and shivering. Her cheekbones slow and sloping and beautiful under those eyes, huge and dark, enchanted, haunting.

Her eyes had caught his for only a moment.

Those dark orbs, doomed, caught his and in an instant, he knew.

It was her.

It was her.

And in a second, a split second, the soldier's shot rang out, against her head.

And she was gone.

But he knew.

In that moment.

It was her.

It was.

And she had slipped, once more, through his grasp.

"You have no idea," the Arimathean said.

"We have been attempting for a long while to locate him, to locate the nexus, but even with our power, they have managed to keep it hidden," Xerxes said. "We were able to discover that it is in this general area, but that is the best we could do, even with all efforts, earthen and otherwise."

"They are powerful as well," the Arimathean said. "Never forget that."

"Of course," Xerxes said. "I only hope, pray, that they have not managed to fully open the gate."

"They have not," the Arimathean said. "Trust me. I have been inside a hellgate. You would know."

Xerxes nodded. He considered, but did not dare to ask.

"The holocaust of blood and souls they sacrificed has not been enough for them," the Arimathean said. "But they are close. And even one more dead is already far too many."

"It is just a blessing they weren't able to locate any of the sarcophagi," Xerxes said.

"They have," the Arimathean said. "Two. But our forces have stopped them from transporting them here, which is the only thing that has kept them from the resurrections."

The Arimathean paused, his forehead pursed in concentration.

"What they have managed to drag forth into this dimension has been wretched enough," he said.

Xerxes stopped, pulled a small circular instrument from his pocket, held it up and watched it glitter against the trickle of light from the heavens.

"The stone," Xerxes said. "The one the eastern star . . . "

"Yes, we are close," the Arimathean said.

They approached a small, otherwise non-descript hill.

"This is it."

They pushed aside a pile to get to the entrance.

A pile.

A pile of bodies, their skin cold, their faces frozen in agony.

The different colors of their uniforms rendered moot by the one color the tattered shards now shared.

Blood red.

They too were men, once. Once.

Now they were little more than an impediment, easily cast aside, the Arimathean thought, like so many others in his past, so many other killing fields like this one.

Too many.

It took them but a few moments to uncover the hidden latch, lifting it up and watching as a portion of the ground pushed aside, the camouflage exposed to reveal a dark stairway leading down, into the bowels of this unholy earth.

Xerxes once more retrieved the glittering object from his pocket.

"This will provide us with some light," he said.

"I don't need it now," the Arimathean said. "I can see."

Xerxes raised an eyebrow and sighed, holding the object up before him to illuminate his path.

"I, on the other hand, will be careful not to alert them to our presence," he said.

"No need," the Arimathean said. "He knows we're here."

"But how?"

"The same way I knew he was," the Arimathean said. "We've known each other a while."

"Then what do we do?" Xerxes said.

"Stay behind me," the Arimathean said.

"If you insist," Xerxes said, eagerly stepping behind as they descended the stairs, coming to a stop before a huge, ornate metal door adorned with ancient sigils and images carved into it. On the top corners of the door were torches, hung from rusty metal claws, burning low, revealing a phrase, written in blood, upon the wall, in an ancient language.

"What does it say?" Xerxes said.

"You don't want to know," the Arimathean said.

The Arimathean's hands gently passed over the sigils upon the door, and for a moment he winced, then caught himself and his eyes became dark.

"What is it?" asked Xerxes.

"It has begun," the Arimathean said, through a stony gaze, cold and dark smoldering in his eyes of burned sienna and gold.

"What does it mean?" Xerxes asked.

"That we need to get through the door."

The Arimathean once again placed his hand up against the cold steel standing between them and their quarry, closed his eyes and concentrated for a few moments, letting his consciousness expand, seeing beyond them, beyond the door.

Until the silence was broken by the sound of muffled voices, frantic, on the other side of the door.

"Stand to the side, quickly," the Arimathean said, nodding to Xerxes as they both pressed against the crumbling walls away from the portal.

The sound of machine gun fire rang out, smashing against the metal in a torrent of steel stings.

Silence.

The Arimathean paused, concentrated, closed his eyes.

Again, the bullets swarmed furious against the inside of the door, some of them shrieking through it, past the two men.

Silence.

The Arimathean looked at Xerxes, nodded. Xerxes slung his machine gun around his shoulder and into his hands. As for the Arimathean, he had no need for such a weapon, as his pulled a huge, brilliant silver katana sword from a scabbard upon his back. The Trinity Blade.

With a quick move, the Arimathean shot his leg into the portal, kicking the door down with superhuman force, sending it firing across the room and momentarily stunning those inside.

The seconds of shock gave them more than enough time.

The soldiers' bullets rang out but with superhuman speed, the Arimathean's blade whirled to block every metal sting from striking him and Xerxes, sending some ricocheting back into the flesh of those who shot them. As the Arimathean's blade dispensed its deadly justice and blocked them from harm, Xerxes stepped out from behind him and opened fire upon the soldiers within, cutting all of them down and sending them crumpling to the floor.

The man they had come for was twisted and shaded, hissing curses, standing at the end of the room. He threw a tiny ebony glass bottle to the floor, shattering it. A crimson flame shot upward and doused the room with smoke and ash, and from the ashes leapt a dozen figures, long wraiths, black bodied with faces of pallid death. Their tentacles slicked with slime protruding like worms vomiting from their pale, bulging lips, and eyes small, round, beady and blood red, with long claws that slashed at the two men who had broken through the door.

They were the Derodiata. Or at least their spirit familiars in this dimension, bereft of hosts.

Xerxes instinctively shrank back for a moment at the sight of the demons, but the Arimathean remained undeterred and unafraid. He had seen them before. Battled them before. With a blur, he sheathed his steel and his fist went to his belt. He pulled out a shiny black scabbard engraved with silver sigils, and with one thought from him, it erupted in a massive fang of blue flame.

The holy sword of justice, a living blade of S'iam B'ala.

Soulsfire.

He carved a deadly tapestry of destruction through the air with the flaming sword, keeping the demons at bay, and then with a few lightning fast swings he sliced through them, disintegrating them, and sending them howling back to the netherworlds from whence they were summoned.

When the demons had fallen back to ash, the men saw their quarry had sheltered himself deeper into the seemingly endless bunker, behind three strange cocoons that looked like massive cockroach eggs, shimmering burnt brown and black, that split open like oozing wounds to reveal a trio of even more grotesque and bizarre creatures, reptilian humanoids, black and scaly, with ragged horns ringing heads dominated by sinister slits of mouths violent with horrible, razor-sharp teeth. They leapt forward upon the men with a frenzy, slashing at them with huge, thick claws that sliced through their uniforms and flesh leaving harsh, deep cuts.

Xerxes tried to fire his gun at them, to no avail, and he would have quickly succumbed and been devoured had it not been for the power of the Arimathean's attack.

Only the holy blade of Soulsfire had any effect upon them, gouging out chunks of their reptilian flesh and leaving it dripping hissing blood to the ground.

With a herculean swing, one was beheaded, then another, and then, finally, the holy sword stabbed mightily through the body of the third, nearly cutting it in two.

Wounded, bathed in blood, and sweat, the Arimathean stepped over the gasping, fallen body of Xerxes. With a look of pure hatred carved upon his face, he stalked to the twisted man they had come for, who was backed against a wall. The demon within the man had, for the moment, receded, and all that remained of this husk was the human, the pathetic wretch who had opened himself up to the otherworldly evil years ago, as part of an occult ritual, under the glow of a full moon. He ground his teeth together and he looked upon the Arimathean with fear and violence. The Arimathean's gaze was acidic and terrible towards him, this man who had murdered so many, had destroyed the lives of millions, this pale, flaccid creature of hatred.

Desperate, in a pathetic attempt, the man raised a gun and shot six times, emptying his cartridge, but with otherworldly speed and reflexes, the Arimathean swung his sword of flame and blocked and disintegrated each bullet. The man reached into his belt for another weapon but the Arimathean easily sliced off the man's hand with one quick swing. As the man squealed in pain, the Arimathean smashed his iron fist into the man's face, sending him sprawling against the wall, to his knees, spitting blood.

He was a man of average height and build, nothing remarkable to look at, but with a distinct air to him, and a palpable weight of malevolence and arrogance to his being. His face was pale and pudgy, his hair dark and stringy, fallen asymmetrically as a sweaty bang over his forehead to one side of his face, framing the burning crimson within his eyes. His teeth were brown and stained beneath a thick nose and a slight rectangle of mustache perched imperiously above his fish-like maw.

He wore a uniform, like the rest, like the other men they had killed to get to this place.

Dark gray.

Black.

With red trim.

And emblazoned with a bastardized symbol.

Once a symbol of light and eternity, one seen throughout the land which laid below the Golden City, the earthen throne of S'iam B'ala, the sacred spires of Tibet.

Now inverted and perverse, forever corrupted with the poison of this man and his followers.

Never to be forgotten.

As a symbol of pain, of evil.

The swastika.

"Hitler," Xerxes said, as he struggled to rise.

"Do not call him that," the Arimathean said. "That is only the shell. Call him instead by the one inside him, pulling the strings."

The Arimathean stepped closer to the German dictator and looked into his eyes, through them, to the demon inside.

"Call him Satanus," the Arimathean said.

Upon the demon's name being called out, the face of Hitler grew a harsh red, his eyes a deep black, and the demon emerged in the human's countenance, a full symbiote of human and otherworldly evil. With a scream from its hideous lips, twin blasts of hellfire burst from its eyes to destroy the one who dared to contain him within word.

But the Arimathean could not be destroyed. Immortal and immersed in the power of the infinite, he held his ground, lifting his sacred sword and drawing the massive burst of demon flame into it, shielding himself and Xerxes until the demon had nearly exhausted its human host and the flame dissipated, leaving the room reeking in an acrid stench and the human shell spent and gray.

With a scowl on his face, the Arimathean strode towards the Hitler-Satanus symbiote.

"You may destroy the cage, but not the beast within," the demon hissed through Hitler's lips as the body rose to its feet. "And this vessel has served its purpose to unleash those you will never cage, who will follow and accompany me…"

The man-demon smirked.

"…as should you, Josephus of Arimathea."

The Arimathean halted for just a moment at the sound of his name coming from the demon.

"How many times will we go through this vain battle, with you killing my human throne, only to see me return, invited once more to take over another human host? How long will you wait, in vain, for another Christ to arrive?" the demon spoke in sleek tones through Hitler's lips. "Another millennium? Two? And all as you watch humanity destroy itself, battling for their petty so-called gods you and I both know are no more than I.

Watch them fight, blind and ignorant, all as you waste your life battling to save humanity from itself, save it from a war it chose, a battle it constantly fights among itself and has millennia before even you were born."

"Do not listen to him!" Xerxes said, calling through agony as he struggled to rise, bleeding and pained. "He cannot be allowed to remain here to poison this world!"

The demon-Hitler symbiote turned to Xerxes and laughed through bloodied lips, turning back to the Arimathean.

"I poison this world?" the demon cackled. "You trust this one, Josephus? He and the Silent Hand? The same men who have manipulated you, used you as little more than a weapon for their own purposes for centuries? Have you noticed, Josephus, our meetings have become fewer and fewer over the years? I don't even need to manifest. These humans, he, and their kind, are all too willing to take up my ways for their own selfish gain, their own greed and hate. And all the while what you call your soul bleeds away, watching those you love die repeatedly as you stand by helpless, dying inside slowly for a God who doesn't care, for a messiah that never arrives, as religions you and I both know are false and hollow occupy these sheep with violent lies."

The eyes of Hitler grew red and a black sea swirled within them as he held out his hand.

"Join me, Josephus, not as my throne, but as my equal, so we may both assume the power we deserve as rulers of this planet," the demon-Hitler symbiote said. "Join me, so that we may rule those who have been summoned to follow, the others who once bowed to me and will again, as this world is crushed to our fist."

"Others?" the Arimathean said.

"This shell and his minions have served me well, for they have begun to open the portals for those to follow," the demon-human said. "And follow they will, as they did in millennia past. Join me, and we will rule them! They will bow to us both!"

"He lies!" Xerxes said. "He will possess and kill you as surely as the one whose body he infests!"

"And who are these who will follow?" the Arimathean said.

The eyes of the Hitler-demon symbiote were fiery as he smiled broadly.

"The ones these humans have worshiped since their time began," the demon-human said. "The old gods. The Archons. The Demiurge."

The Arimathean tensed at their mention and the demon symbiote smirked.

"Our sorcery, our science, has gravely wounded The Black Knight. It has been crippled and is being slowly destroyed. Before a century passes it will have died. Its creators have abandoned you. The Annunaki are no more. The Elohim, the Watchers, have disappeared with the Magi. These ignorant humans can do nothing to restore the satellite. The Thule has succeeded, the Nephilim will once more walk the earth. And once the artifacts are ours once more, the Nephilim will open the gates for the old gods to resume their thrones and conquer this world beside them," the Hitler-demon coughed violently, doubled over, then raised up again, as the smell of sulfur began to fill the room. "And I, upon my throne, will lead them!"

Once more, he held out his hand to the Arimathean.

"Join me, so we may rule together as the gods we truly are, over these pathetic sheep who were born to worship us!"

The Arimathean reached out and grasped the demon-human's hand.

"Do not let him!" Xerxes cried, wincing through his pain.

As the Arimathean locked hands with the symbiote, he felt not only the demon-human's hand cold and clasping like a steel trap, he felt a frigid grasp tighten about him, as the demon began to leave his human host in anticipation of possessing the Arimathean's body.

But as the demon's spirit oozed from Hitler, and the stench of sulfur permeated the room, the Arimathean pulled the demon-human symbiote tight to him so it could not escape, and then, with his other hand, grasped the scabbard of Soulsfire, ignited the blue flame of the holy sword and buried it deep into the body of the Hitler-Satan symbiote.

The body convulsed as it began to smolder and ignite in a violet pyre, the flesh and bone of Hitler crumbling as Satan's essence clung tenaciously to it, grasped desperately to avoid being cast from the earthen plane by the power of Soulsfire.

But before it was dispelled, the demon-human smiled at the Arimathean and looked deep into his eyes.

"There is a part of you that knows already you are not choosing between good and evil," the demon smiled, "but between the lesser of two evils. And they are closer to each other than you know."

The Arimathean scowled and threw the smoldering husk of body to the ground, but the two red portals where its eyes once were continued to hold his gaze in their sinister grasp as the demon faded away.

"We will meet again, and you will know the true prince of lies is not I," the demon purred as it faded to dark and its words echoed behind it. "Enjoy your prison, Josephus..."

His face sour, teeth clenched, the Arimathean brought the sword down again on the body, engulfing it in flame, but it was dead, the demon already gone, only its words remaining.

The Arimathean looked around the room, at the soldiers freshly killed, at the disgusting tableau of ritual sacrifices Hitler and his acolytes had performed before their arrival, their bodies hollow and drained.

Lives.

Each of them born to this planet seemingly innocent.

Somehow, someway, poisoned and tarred along the way.

And now, gone.

Why?

"That was wise, my friend," Xerxes said, with a strange, hopeful, yet suspicious tone. "Feigning collaboration to gain information."

The Arimathean said nothing.

Again, he looked around the room, searching.

Until he saw what he had come to obtain.

Cloaked in blood, held in a ritual cask behind the fallen flesh of Hitler.

He lifted the harsh, jagged steel artifact, heavy and ancient, from the cask, and felt a rush of power through him. For a moment, he held it, tightly, and then, placed it, still dripping with blood, into the large velvet and silver pouch he had brought to contain it.

"Is that the blade, the spear?" Xerxes said, incredulous.

The Arimathean nodded, sealing the pouch as he murmured a prayer and felt an electricity scald his hand, burning, burning, until it faded and cooled, and the pouch grew feather light despite the weight of its cargo.

"So, they have . . ."

The Arimathean merely glanced at him, and Xerxes knew.

He strode to Xerxes, held out his hand and lifted the injured warrior to his feet, propping him up and helping him up and away from the bunker, still reeking of sulfur, still dripping with death.

They walked up the stairs and were greeted by darkness, silence, the crimson moon still ominously hanging like a scythe, illuminating the same grim garden of destruction which surrounded them as they walked once more, through the valley of lifeless bodies, across the cruel, barren earth.

And as they did, the ground shook briefly, and the moon went darker, the color of dead blood, and a cascade of stars fell through the ebon skies, disintegrating as they made their way towards earth.

"What does that mean?" Xerxes said.

"That this is the beginning," the Arimathean said, "the beginning of the end."

# ONE

**Toronto**

**New Year's Eve, 1999**

"You sure you're leaving?"

Tabitha leaned her dangerously curved body, hugged in a tight black dress, against the wall just next to the glowing button for the elevator, her red lips mystery hooked in a smile below mischievous brown eyes and dark Bettie Page bangs.

"You sure you don't want to stick around, ring in the new year with me?" she smirked, raising an eyebrow. "I'll make it worth your while."

Akira chuckled slightly, looking boyish in his tight-fitted dark gray pants and tie, light gray shirt fitted tight around his lithe body, his raven shock of hair curved slightly over his high cheekbones, olive skin and wide smile.

"Somehow, I'm guessing my girlfriend wouldn't be happy with that," Akira said.

"She doesn't need to know," Tabitha said, biting her lower lip. "After all, look at where we work. I think we're obviously well versed in keeping secrets."

"Yes, we are, and I'm very flattered, but . . . no," Akira said, sighing, and running his hand through the dark waves of his hair and returning her smile.

"Well," she said, "why don't you stick around anyway, just to celebrate our victory for keeping civilization alive. Or, what passes for it, anyway."

The elevator door opened.

"No, thanks," Akira said. "Again, I appreciate the invitation. But with everything going on, I'm exhausted. I haven't slept in weeks."

"Well, I wouldn't want to keep you up any longer," she said, raising an eyebrow and prowling, cat-like towards him, rubbing just against him as she passed by, allowing him to catch her scent as she slunk back to the party.

"Happy new year, Akira," she purred, "thanks for helping to save the world."

Akira chuckled and smiled. He looked back, thought for a moment, then exhaled and walked into the elevator as it opened.

"Hey!" the heavy-set man on his phone called to Akira as he ran towards the door.

Akira pressed the button and the doors stopped and re-opened as the man nodded a thank you.

The doors slid slowly shut.

Akira pressed a button and looked to the man, still on his phone.

"Yeah, I'm lower level too, garage too," the man said towards Akira, then returned to his phone, "Uh huh. Yeah. Yeah. Ok."

He hung up.

The elevator began its descent.

"You on the Y2K team?" he asked Akira.

"Yes."

"Pretty amazing job you guys did."

"Thank you."

"It's just incredible, when you think about it, that just this little code could've had such a huge impact on everything."

"Well, it's a little more complex than that."

"Always is, huh?" the man smiled.

Akira returned his smile. "Yes, it always is."

The man leaned against the wall, still looking at Akira.

"So, everything is fixed now and everything, right?"

"Yes," Akira said.

"But, be honest, was it ever that big a deal to begin with?" the man said.

"It could've been," Akira said. "Thankfully, we'll never know."

"Yeah, prevention is always best in the big picture," the man said, in a way that made Akira feel strange.

The man's demeanor shifted back into jovial mode.

"You know, I was listening to the radio the other day, one of those conspiracy theory talk shows or something, and there was some guy saying that the whole Y2K bug was just a hoax. Just some new world order thing to keep tabs on people, to locate aliens that had infiltrated the population or something like that."

"How so?" Akira scrunched his face, quizzically.

"Like with the DNA thing, and all the cameras, all the facial recognition technology," the man said. "Now that everybody is on the computer, and everybody is becoming more connected, it's becoming easier for the governments to locate anyone they want, at any time, and harder for people to be hidden or have any privacy."

"That's . . . an interesting theory," Akira said, subconsciously shuffling a bit towards the wall, away from the man.

The man burst wide into a loud guffaw.

"Man, that stuff is hilarious, there are so many crazy theories out there, ya know?"

"Yeah."

The door opened to the lower level, to the dark shadows of the garage area, lined with dim halogen lights.

Akira stood by the elevator door, blocking it, and allowing the man to leave the compartment first.

The man nodded, walked out, reached into his pocket, then turned around.

"Hey, thanks a lot, Akira!"

Akira nodded to him. "You're welcome," he said, then realized, "Wait, how did you know my . . . ?"

"Capulet knows all," the man said coldly, as the tranquilizer dart shot quickly from his gun.

But to Akira's surprise, he, by reflex alone, hurtled back against the elevator wall and managed to dodge the projectile fired at him.

"Damn it!" the man swore, as Akira leapt from the elevator and tackled him.

The man fell, hard, to the concrete, the back of his head smacking against the ground. He yelled out in pain and dropped his gun. Akira quickly leapt up just in time to see two other men raising tranquilizer guns and firing at him. The darts soared towards him, but again, he was able to slip out of their trajectory as they crashed against the concrete walls.

The first man had recovered and attempted another shot, but it went wide, and Akira was able to compose himself and run behind a row of cars to shield himself. The three men ran after him and Akira could hear the clatter of their shoes against the concrete.

And then he heard their screams.

One. Another. And the third. A quick blurt of pain, followed by a gurgle, and then, the sound of their bodies hitting the ground.

Akira stopped.

Peered around the side of a van.

Then felt the hand close around his neck from behind.

Instinctively, without even realizing what he was doing, his body flew into a dazzling ballet of violence. He grasped the arm of the being behind him, twisting it into a grotesque angle at incredible speed, then three quick blows to the head and body of the black-clad figure followed by a swirling kick that sent the being smashing into the concrete wall.

Akira looked down at the being and his mind began to explode with images, memories, a torrent of his past lives a hurricane through his brain as he looked down to see the prone being, unconscious on the ground.

He had never seen anything like it before. It had the shape of a man, but in a skin-tight black suit that shimmered like metal, and a helmet wrapped around its head, with two huge almond shaped eyes that shined like glass visors. But most disturbing was the insignia above the right breast, and upon its right shoulder. Blood red. Unmistakable.

A swastika.

Stunned, his mind suddenly slowed, and it all became lucid for him.

Who he really was.

And why he was here.

Too late.

He remembered the beings behind him.

Spun around.

And felt the green, glowing blade rip through him.

Saw the face of the one who drove it into his chest.

He was a towering, over seven foot, wire of a man, with inky hair pulled back from his face. The claw of a tight widow's peak carved into his massive forehead, over razor cheekbones and jawbone molded in steel. He was beautiful and sinister. He had a shark-like countenance, eyes black, soulless, and devoid of any kindness, and within his wicked mouth were twin rows of sharpened teeth. He was clad like the other Reichtarg, in the black uniform, but without a mask. Surrounded by eight others like the one stunned on the ground. All of them surrounding Akira. All of them circling the man who twisted the strange knife, glowing with green sigils as it drenched with Akira's blood and sucked it into its grooves, as it glowed brighter, brighter, as the blood filled it. The man held Akira up, keeping the blade in his chest, held by the being's six fingers clasped around the perverse emerald fang, as he looked deep into Akira's eyes.

"Please tell me you remember me," the man said. "This won't be anywhere near as satisfying if you don't remember anything . . ."

And then, as his life began to drain from him, Akira struggled to push away, but the beings swarmed him and held him tight to the blade.

And Akira remembered.

He remembered who he was.

And who this being was as well.

"Shernihaza."

The being smiled wide with jagged malevolence.

"Yes, thank you for remembering . . . Melchior," he hissed, shoving the sword into the reincarnated Magi's body and up, running him through and feeling his dying essence leave his shell.

The bleeding body slid off Shernihaza's blade and fell to the ground. Dead.

Shernihaza knelt over it and shook his head slowly.

"I expected this to be so much more rewarding," the leader of the Nephilim sighed, surrounded by the cadre of Reichtarg. "I hope the next Magi is at least a little more of a challenge."

Shernihaza drove the blade back into Melchior's chest, allowing it to drain the body of blood.

Behind him, a large, shambling figure slunk forward. It was hunched and grotesque, covered in bandages and enchanted salves to keep it alive, its flesh putrid and stinking, its voice hissing and sinister.

The Babylonian.

He looked down at Melchior's dead body, now pale and dry.

"The Blade of Drago . . . "The Babylonian hissed. ". . . give it to me."

Shernihaza pulled it from the body of the fallen Magi, and it glowed with the blood and power of the reincarnated holy warrior it had just extinguished. The Nephilim demon handed it to The Babylonian.

Instantly upon touching it, The Babylonian began to grow stronger, stronger, his body expanding, his wounds healing, as he pulsed with the new power of such an elite and supernatural sacrifice.

"Yes . . . yes . . ." The Babylonian hissed, his voice growing stronger, his eyes glowing crimson and gold. "This shall sustain me in this dimension, until the artifacts, and the others can be found."

The blade drained of all energy by the Demiurge, its color went to an inky emerald, its glow vanished. The Babylonian handed it back to Shernihaza, who sheathed it.

They looked back at the dead body of the Magi, and with a gesture from Shernihaza, a bolt of fire erupted from the Nephilim's hand and flew to Melchior's body, engulfing it in flame and burning it to ash.

And then the cadre of evil slipped into a line of long, jet black limousines, and they slowly cruised, like panthers leaving devoured prey, out into the night.

# TWO

**New York City**

**2042**

The sleek, scaly claws of darkness held tight around the barren neighborhood in the diseased side of town.

It was near 4 a.m., the hour of the wolf.

The neighborhood was alive only behind locked doors and barred windows. The streets were bare as bones licked clean by vermin. Fear and distraction held its occupants inside as soon as the merest hint of darkness began to slip through the streets like the foul uninvited hands of a stranger.

Most of them escaped as quickly as possible after they had locked themselves in. Put on their visi-pods and disappeared into the virtual world, most with the accompaniment of their own legal opiates to help glide them past consciousness until they next had to wake upon sunlight. Sustenance was usually gained in a form of Nutrio, via pill or liquid, a cheap chemical blend of vitamins, minerals, carbohydrates, mood stabilizers and proteins keeping them compliant, alive, enough to work, enough to maintain the status quo for those above them. And so was life for most. An existence of transport from cage to cage, sustaining themselves on processed nourishment both physical and mental.

And, ultimately, emotional. Brains lit up by inconsistent rewards of beeps and lights via connections on social media and pre-programmed affirmations thrown their way through the web, when their chips indicated they needed more serotonin or dopamine.

There were some who had escaped. Some who resided in the free-range zones. Who lived off nature. Who had learned to. Who had formed cells which had disengaged from the web, from the microchipped society.

But that wasn't here. Not in the cities.

There was little in the way of an edifice that wasn't scarred by some form of graffiti, and few that weren't pocked by the remnants of some missed shot or scar from some weapon, some fight long past, but never bothered to be healed. Garbage piled along the streets. Budget tightening forcing the frequency of the robotized collection trucks to be dulled down to once a month at best in some areas.

Areas like this.

The drones wove their way silently overhead, through the maze of streets, as data from the chipped population bounced upwards to them. Locations. Key words of dialogue. Electromagnetic signatures that signaled emotion, interaction, chemical variation . . . that signaled any triggers to the Argus web above.

Low level waves bounced down from the drones and the satellites, again, making sure the chips were functioning as intended. Making sure they were functioning within each being, exercising their control. To quell the population, to prevent contraception, to keep it from overpopulating, to monitor it, ostensibly for its safety, to keep those inside safe . . . from those who weren't.

Out in the streets, in these segments of the city, street lights were shot out or hacked and reprogrammed for darkness to cloak those dealing in illegal contraband and drugs. And while the drones could see in the ultraviolet, those monitoring cared little about what they caught. Best to keep the masses quelled and cowed with the chemicals to keep them down, no harm in letting them tighten the nooses about their own necks.

What little light existed in these shot out wastelands was provided by the street signals, holograms whose codes were much harder to hack, unable to be shot out and turned to puddles of falling glass raining onto the odorous puddles and scampering vermin below.

The small vermin.

And the larger animals.

The packs of the un-chipped.

Scars down their arms and across the backs of their necks from where the implants had been removed, by them or their pack. Marks and faces covered in violent holograms. Teeth filed to fangs and eyes stained dark by overuse of the Kryo.

The Kryo. The synthetic drug which kept them taut and vicious, kept them scything through the streets like bodies of piranha looking for their next score and the victims to provide it, to provide the credits for it.

They killed and tortured at will with little thought or care of retribution. Stripping their victims bare of possessions and dignity, torturing them, and ultimately cannibalizing them. They were little more than wild animals. Unregistered children, unauthorized conceptions thrown to the streets to keep their parents from jail time for unlicensed reproduction, left to fight to survive, often on the blood of others within the same pool of human detritus.

They were kept electronically caged in these ghettos by the gatekeepers and drones which protected the more upscale neighborhoods, those who paid more in tax, more in protection money. The police and drones ringed the perimeters of the better neighborhoods and did not hesitate to shoot to kill the anti-chipped packs of the vicious who dared to venture beyond their ghettos into more affluent territory. But there were too many of the packs and not enough police, and so certain areas of the city were given up once the sun went down.

While those in authority gave grandiose speeches about changing the system and remedying the solution, little was done but to work to confine the packs to the areas where only the poor and voiceless were forced to eke out an existence locked in fear.

Those unwise enough to walk these streets at night invariably ended up dead, or worse.

And usually undiscovered, or given much effort at discovery.

It was amidst this morass, the woman walked, alone.

Unafraid.

She cut a steely, imposing figure as she strode through the inky streets. She was clad in a sleek, metallic silver armor and black leather and synthetic suit that slid around the curves of her muscular form. Slung around her waist was a belt featuring a variety of small compartments and pouches and two prominent blasters. Across her back was a huge kitana sword. And wrapped around her head was the death mask of her warrior tribe. A black, metallic visage with slanted, cold, almond shaped eye visors, a series of transmission and cloaking spikes, large to small, flaring back from the crown on both sides and, just below the eye on the left side, three red slashes, in honor of one who had founded their order.

The order of the Sikari.

She found the dimly-lit warehouse wall she was looking for, pressed a sequence on the clandestine pad embedded into the brick and watched as a shimmering steel portal opened from the decaying red stone facade. She entered, into a small, dimly lit holo-bar, filled with doomed skeletons of men and women slumped forward and locked in, tubes of inebriate needled into their arms and virtual helmets locked in about their heads as they floated through worlds far from here. A few remained unleashed to the Virtua. The guardians, those paid to protect the bodies of those strapped in to the system. And a few others, who lacked the credits for the web, who were left to escape in other ways, still barely lucid, their heads bowed over their drinks on tables dimly lit in the foggy, errant scraps of fluorescence above them.

In a murky corner sat two. One man, older, but hard to tell exactly as Kryo had hollowed him. He was a tall, rat-like human, hair greasy and long, pulled back at odd angles and wrapped in bands. Skin pale and scabbed. Cheeks sunken, eyes shallow and glassy. And a woman. Young. Just on the edge of her teens, perhaps early twenties. Small and thin, with huge violet eyes rung wide in black eye makeup, dark purple lips, cherubic white face, and dark hair shorn short and severe on the sides with a thick multi-colored cascade untamed on the top. They were both clad darkly in oversized jackets lined with anti-magnetic material and circuitry to hide their cargo, and, when their hoods were zipped over them, to cloak them from the drones.

"Do you think it was the Russians?" the man said.

"No," the woman said.

"Why not?" the man said.

"Because they thought it was us."

"And because they were as scared as we were," he said, bobbling his foot quickly and tapping his fingers on the table.

"Scared?" she said, taking a drink of a blue, glowing liquid from a glass beaker. "I didn't get a scared vibe from them. I thought they were curious."

"Curious?"

"But curiosity usually has fear at its root," she said. "So, maybe."

The Sikari approached the table, causing both to jolt upright.

She briefly exposed her left palm to them and a computer chip within it flashed a number.

The tall man sat up, licked his lips, raised his hand to his chin. Breathed out. Nodded.

The woman nodded.

The woman raised her palm to the Sikari, and a rectangular hologram appeared bearing a maze of patterns and numbers.

They shook hands and a brief jolt of low level electricity passed between them, giving them both a brief halo of warmth over their hands, as the information they held was simultaneously encrypted and transferred to remote locations for verification.

The Sikari sat down. With merely a thought from her, the organic circuitry of her mask responded and it seemed to melt away, pooling and forming into a thick halo around her neck. She was revealed as a stunning woman with olive skin and long, silken dark hair braided back tight to her head. She had high, severe cheekbones, full lips, a dangerous, exotic beauty and huge, dark eyes, the color of the earth at the sun's daily death, with flecks of gold dancing within them.

As her face was revealed, she noticed the rat-like man jolt back a bit in recognition, before nervously attempting to compose himself.

She knew.

And her consciousness began to scatter about the room.

"Now we wait, huh?" the rat-like man said. "Yeah."

The Sikari merely sat silently.

"What do you think? Huh? The Athena. What do you think happened?" the rat-like man scattered. "We, I, think it was the Russians. You know, I know, you know, I mean, we all know, what it was doing, where it was going, and why. I mean, Mars, do you really think? I mean, do you think it really disappeared? Or do you think they're just saying that to cover up?"

The Sikari remained silent.

The rat-like man looked at the other woman, who had been waiting there with him.

"What do you think again?" he said, skittishly.

"I don't know," she said, uncomfortably. "I seem to recall just telling you that a whole two minutes ago."

The Sikari looked at the woman.

"What do you think?" the woman said to the Sikari.

"I don't think," the Sikari said. "I know."

The woman tilted her head, slightly quizzical, as she felt a slight twinge in her head, strange, like an eggshell crackling, briefly, then she was clear.

The rat-like man looked at the Sikari, stoic, the latter's eyes piercing the rat-like man's. The tall, pale man began to fidget even more, the Kryo he had flooded into his system less than 15 minutes ago beginning to kick in, and as it did, he began to feel something, like the touch of fingers across his brain, and the fear, the fear grabbed across him like a cold steel glove.

The Sikari looked at the two of them.

"What do you know?" the rat-like man asked, staring across the table at the stony face of the armored woman.

The Sikari's eyes slanted as she scanned between the pair.

"I know you are Sintaras Zynt, a petty degenerate and killer, hardly worth my time," she said, looking at the sweating, rat-faced man, before looking towards the woman. "And you, I know who you are, even more than you."

"What's that supposed to mean?" the girl said. "Extra points for Cryptic House?"

"You were born far from here, brought to this country as a child and raised in a free-range zone, but you fled, to become a mercenary and thief not long ago. You were born of one name, and now you call yourself another, Zinesha Faron."

"What . . .how did you know that?" the woman tried to remain nonchalant but her eyes widened.

The Sikari smirked at her. "Is that curiosity I see, or fear?"

Zinesha slid back in her chair away from the table.

"I know you haven't worked together long," the Sikari said to them both. "You met by chance, or so she thinks, finding the same treasure . . . while trying to steal something else . . . with neither of you having any real idea of what you found, only knowing it would be valuable to someone like me, who would meet with you in secret, with a lot of money."

The Sikari looked squarely at Sintaras.

"And that I would be worth a lot more money."

The woman curved slightly in her chair. "How did . . . "

"She's a Magi, a Sikari," the rat-like man said, biting his lips, as the sweat began to bead on his forehead. "The daughter of the most powerful Magi, the Arimathean. Her name is Bastian Ki."

"But I thought . . ." the woman said.

"You did," Bastian said to the woman, then looked over at the rat-faced man, and added, "and you, did not."

Bastian leaned forward towards him. "Tell me," she said, "if you knew my life was worth so much, what made you think yours wouldn't be worth so little in exchange?"

The sweating man snapped, the fear commanding him to attack, and the thought of it flashed into his head, the commands from his brain to his hands to grab his gun at the speed of his dull electrical current.

But not quicker than Bastian Ki.

With a flash, the Sikari's blaster was drawn and shot, a bloom of white light beneath the table, and the rat-like man dropped, cold, face first onto the hard surface. Dead.

Zinesha's hand went to her weapon but Bastian Ki was already ahead of her, getting into her brain and cutting off the electrical impulses to Zinesha's arm, making it fall, limp, to her side. Another quick move and Bastian grabbed Zinesha's other arm and pulled her close to her.

"The Thule have a reaction time of two seconds, tops," Bastian hissed. "They didn't expect this, so you have maybe one, two more seconds to make it to that far right corner. Go!"

Zinesha didn't hesitate, bolting from the table and diving towards the ground beneath a table in the far right corner of the holo-bar. As she did, the table behind her exploded in a torrent of blaster fire from the men masquerading as guardians standing on the other end of the holo-bar.

The Thule had been disguised, but the pretense was past.

But Bastian had already known, already scanned the thoughts of those in the room. Finding blank spots where she knew bodies to be, knowing well the Thule could, like her, cloak their presence, she had calculated the number of Thule and their positions.

Utilizing one of the transportation stones within her belt, she teleported away from the table and to the ceiling a split-second before the blaster fire erupted, and using the anti-gravity magnetic field built into her armor, she ran across the ceiling upside down, blasters pulled and raining down destruction with lethal precision, quickly cutting down the Thule while sparing those innocents around them, still unaware, doped and somnambulant, locked into the Virtua.

Her enemies fresh smudges on the floor, she scrambled down the far wall to the ground and called to Zinesha.

"Come with me or die!" the Sikari said.

Zinesha ran to her side. "Not much of a choice," she said.

"Stay behind me, and close," Bastian said. "There are ten outside, and they have a hovercraft. Stay close! You won't teleport with me otherwise!"

Zinesha nodded. "Staying close, no problem."

Bastian shot the door open, firing with both blasters, and then, with a flash, as the Thule reacted and returned fire, she and Zinesha disappeared, reappearing in the hovercraft.

With lightning speed, Bastian pulled her kitana sword and decapitated the two Thule within the craft, shoving their bodies aside and taking the controls. Her fingers moved across the board and blaster fire exploded from the front of the craft to the ground, slicing through the Thule who had been waiting outside the holo-bar. Then she took the controls and the hovercraft lifted into the air, away from the crumbling false façade of the holo-bar and towards the outskirts of the city, away from the heart of the grid, into the free-range zones.

"How did you know?" Zinesha said, sitting down, and clutching her bleeding hands that had caught her fall into the far end of the bar. "But . . . I thought the Magi . . . you shot first. . ."

"I did," Bastian replied. "I tend to like it better than getting shot."

"So why did you let him get so close to you?" she said.

"Makes it a lot easier to shoot him, doesn't it?"

"Good point," she said.

"Besides, I'm not Magi. I'm Sikari."

"But he said your father was a Magi . . ."

"He was."

"Is he . . . not?"

"My father follows his own path," Bastian said, as the hovercraft drifted away from the murk of the city lights and towards the starlight and darkness beyond. "And always, ultimately, alone."

# THREE

## Chicago

## 1980

The sun set harshly outside the window, carving shadows into the room. Its crimson and gold throes slashed about the artificial light, casting a dull patina over the pastel tomb.

The rasp of machines competed with the strained breaths of the weak and wrinkled man, strung with tubes, upon the bed.

Next to him sat a younger looking, muscular version of the faded gray figure on the bed, slumped over on a chair pushed next to the bed, as close as it could go. He was dressed in black, standing in stark contrast to the old man's pale gown.

The dark man's hands held the dying man's wrinkled paw.

Caressed the leathery, spotted, pale skin.

Held the fading, drying hand close.

Touched it to his face.

Kissed it, as it was touched by the dark man's tears.

The man in black held the hand of the old man on the bed like a cherished treasure, held it tight, looked into the eyes of the old man, and the man in black began to sob.

"Don't... cry," the old man said, as he reached his other hand over, slowly, in an attempt to console the man in black. "Don't..."

"I... I can't..." the man said. "I'm sorry. I tried . . . I tried . . ."

"I know..." the old man rasped. "You... even you... cannot..."

The old man stopped, coughed.

The man in black put his arm around him and caressed his back softly.

The old man looked up at his face.

The old man had tried as well. He had listened to the man in black. He had tried to be brave.

But he could not help but be sorrowful, could not help but feel . . . afraid.

"Hold me…" the old man said. "Hold me like you did… like you used to…"

The man in black got on the bed and laid down, snuggled in close to the old man, sharing the large bed with him, and he put his arms around him, held him like a child, like a baby, in his arms.

And tears began to stream from the face of the old man.

"Hold me in your big bear hug," the old man said. "Hold me, keep me warm. Like a big bear."

The man in black could not speak.

Tears held his throat captive.

Kept it silent.

"Like a big bear hug…" the old man rasped.

The man in black held him tighter, felt him fading away.

"I… I will see you again," the old man said, smiling softly. "Don't worry… you'll… you'll see me… you'll see her… too… soon…."

The old man's last strength flowed through his chest, into his arms, as he held the man in black tightly, put his head to his chest.

"I love… you…" the old man said.

"I love you too," the man in black said, through tears.

The old man smiled.

And then the old man closed his eyes and his body shrunk, and his spirit passed, a smile still on his face, as he laid in the arms of the man in black.

The man in black felt the man fold into him and he whispered his name.

No response.

He whispered it again, into his ear.

"I love you."

No reply.

He said his name. Again. And again.

But with no reply.

And then he held him closer, tight to him, as tight as he could, as if trying to prevent him from leaving. But it was too late.

He was gone.

And the man in black sobbed.

Softly at first.

And then loudly.

And his cries echoed through the room.

As the sun was gone outside, and darkness set in, and all that illumined the room was the artificial light.

The man in black laid there.

As the sky outside grew darker.

Black.

Impenetrable.

And all that surrounded them was the silence.

The sound of the machines, wheezing in surrender.

And the dead, pale light.

The man in black held him.

Held the body of the dead man next to him.

Held it as the warmth slowly faded away from it.

Held it as he had so many times, over the years.

Held it as he had in this same hospital, so many decades ago.

So warm.

So alive.

And now, so cold.

He held it, for hours, for he knew he would not be disturbed.

His power had bought at least that privacy, that privilege.

And when finally, as the hour turned midnight, as the day turned over, he got up, slowly, and laid the body down, gently.

He looked upon it again.

Touched the dead man's face.

Held his hand to his cheek.

Kissed his lips.

His cheek.

His forehead.

As tears streamed from his eyes.

"I love you," the man in black said. "I always will love you."

He kissed his forehead again.

The same forehead he had kissed so many years before.

"I'll see you again," he said, as he kissed him once more, looked at his face, and walked, slowly, from the room.

He had been through this before.

Too many times.

Far too many.

He strode silently, softly, from the room, towards the desk by the elevator.

The nurses avoided eye contact until he prompted them, with a gesture, with a sound.

"Please leave him," the man in black said. "I will be back."

"Yes sir," the nurse at the desk said.

The man in black strode to the elevator doors, stood in front of their glimmering steel, looked upon his face, his reflection, warped in the twin mirrors, portals to his exit.

Saw the same face he had seen, unlined and unchanged, over the past two-thousand years.

The face of the man who was called by some The One Who Cannot Die.

Who others called by the name he had been known since ancient times.

The Arimathean.

The doors opened.

He entered, alone.

Pressed the button.

Down.

A woman, a nurse, quickly strode towards the elevator door. He pressed the button to hold the door open and she entered, gently smiling at him in thanks, until she noticed his face, red and lined.

Her face went soft, concerned, her large blue eyes wide with compassion.

She looked into the man's burning, teary eyes.

They were striking.

Ethereal.

Dark sienna, the color of the skies and earth meeting at dusk, flecked with brilliant bands of gold.

"I'm very sorry, sir," she said.

"Thank you," the man in black said, softly.

"Was he, your father?" the nurse asked.

"No," the man in black said, removing his hand, and allowing the doors to move again. "He was my son."

And then the doors shut. A reflection in steel, broken by a rift down the middle.

The Arimathean was once more confronted by his visage.

He watched, as the light dimmed in him and his face turned to stone.

How many times had he looked into this face?

Into these eyes?

And seen this same visage.

And how many times would he, again?

# FOUR

**New York City**

**2042**

The night was harsh and oppressive, still cold and brutal, and darkness blanketed the ghetto.

It was barren.

But for two men.

Two men.

One young, one old.

The young, a thick, muscular presence, cloaked in black, from jacket to cowl over his head and shading most of his face.

He was huge and muscular, with dark skin, unforgiving features, long ebon and brown hair pulled back and eyes which glimmered gold and sienna, cut in a menacing slant above his hard nose and stony cheekbones. He strode confidently through the jungle even as he heard the howls and cries of pain in the distance.

Vagrants and deviants hiding amidst the detritus watched as he cut through their realm, but even the most desperate for help and the most cunning seeking victims stayed clear. Something inside them warned them, instinct shooting a gaping wound into their guts by his presence that caused them to stay away. From both.

The old man was a wraith in dark gray, thick coat, shirt and pants, his hair near snow white, yet thick and pulled back from his face, wrinkled, and weathered, but ruggedly handsome, with a sharp nose and cheekbones carving a stern visage, as a leathery scar sliced down one side of his face.

Both had appeared, seemingly from the shadows, to meet on a corner dimly lit by a drone above.

The two stood.

One had been waiting a few moments.

The other had just joined him.

Waiting.

The street lights shot out around them. Only the holographs and signs remaining, flickering in and out.

They stood, in the hand of darkness.

Black night.

An abyss.

Around just one light.

Tiny and seemingly insignificant.

Hovering over the heads of the two men.

A media drone.

The satellite buzzed slightly before it stopped, resting just above the fading sign nearby them. The circuits within the sign purred to life once the drone hovered in proximity to it, activated by a sensor within the drone.

Normally, three tiny computer chips would activate it.

One located in the sign. The other two typically implanted in the men.

But neither man had one.

The drone clicked slightly as it hovered above a "Transit" sign, then emitted a hologram of an attractive brunette woman with light mocha skin and intoxicating cocoa colored eyes. She was sheathed in a tight, tailored navy blue suit over a crisp white shirt. Behind her hovered one large logo of her corporate network, surrounded by other commercial logos which changed every few seconds, depending on how much time the corporations featured in the ads had purchased.

"Hello and welcome to UNN. In tonight's top stories, the crew of the Mars expedition ship Athena remains incommunicado with NASA," the woman began. "The ship, the second sent to the red planet to begin colonization of Mars, lost contact with earth thirty-three days ago, and the fate of the ship and its crew remain unknown."

"Unknown," the older man said, dubiously.

The younger man's eyes slanted and he nodded slightly.

"And in other news, three women were attacked on the east side this morning, with two killed and the other left badly mutilated," the newscaster said. "Police refused to confirm that this was the latest in the trend of local gangs 'feasting' on random victims. Motives for the crimes are unknown, but citizens are encouraged to remain indoors and off the streets after dark and to report any suspicious groups of more than three unknown people to their local authorities.

"And in other news, the international computer hacker Anansi..." the news woman trailed off, as the two men walked a few paces back, to the beaten-up sign hanging over the street, barely illuminated by its solar panel, bearing the word "Transit."

"Savages," the old man said, shaking his head. "All a bunch of savages. The world is such a dirty place. I've been on this God-forsaken planet, oh, too many, years now, and it's never been worse."

The younger man's eyes grew dark and he nodded slightly, scanned the area around them.

The older man, encouraged, nodded.

"Look around us, look at this, this city is in ruins," the older man said. "Lights shot out, the buildings either abandoned or locked up, the windows with bars on them. People in cages, willingly, with no way out but death."

In the distance, they heard voices, breaking glass.

"Then what brings you out?" the younger man said.

"Ah, business, my friend, always business," the older man said, with a nod and wink. "And I've been alive too long to change. I refuse to allow this city, or its occupants, to devour me."

He patted the chest of his coat.

"And I have means to protect me, let us say," the old man winked.

The younger man was silent.

"And what brings you out?" the older man said.

"The same."

The sounds in the distance grew closer, a can being kicked and voices, now low and chuckling.

The old man looked around, then to the younger man next to him. He tried to identify him, but he remained cut in shadow, his features just beyond reach.

He looked to be in his thirties.

Obviously of money, dressed in fine clothing and wrapped in a long, jet black wool coat.

Large. Muscular build.

He wore a dark hood, but beneath it could be seen flashes of dark brown hair, pulled back away from his face, but still long enough to cusp through the lower part of the hood.

His face was coarse and distant. Handsome, but harsh and forbidding.

And his eyes, what the old man could see of his eyes, flashing a second or two before driving back into dark, were eerie, when the dim light cast against them.

Haunted.

"How is it," the old man said, "that the street lights are beaten up, dim and shot out, and the city looks like the depression, but these hovercraft and cameras and media drones can still look pristine?"

"Because nobody cares about the street lights or the city," the younger man said. "The corporations want the media drones and the cameras, so they're magnetically shielded to prevent damage to them."

"But don't the cameras need the lights? Why would they let the lights get shot out?"

"The lights, or their hollow corpses, aren't so that people can see, they're so that people realize they cannot," the younger man said. "If they can see the lights shot out, they stay inside, out of fear. So, the cameras outside aren't needed as much. And even if they were, the cameras shoot in the UV spectrum. They don't need light to film."

The younger man looked around slowly, scanning, as the low laughter and chatter died, the sounds of cans kicked and broken glass being shoved over the pavement gone cold and quiet.

"How do you know all this?" the older man said.

"Because I work for the man who designed them."

The older man looked at the younger man, and began to back slowly away from him.

"That's also how I know your name, Dorin Xerxes," the younger man said.

Xerxes' instinctively reached for his blaster, but the younger man's eyes met his and Xerxes found his arm frozen, found himself unable to move it. He tried to move his other arm to pull a blade, but it too was dead.

As he figured he soon would be as well.

"We know all about you," the younger man said. "We know you live off the grid, hidden in plain sight, using public transportation and public services, but acting inconspicuously to avoid any tracking. You are well over 100 years old, yet you sustain yourself on Silent Hand magicks and neo technology you obtain through the black market and your connections. The same connections you were going to meet tonight. You travel with black market government permits allowing you to use cash, grandfathered in due to your age and your alleged military record, or at least the one claimed on your permits."

"I have… my permits are…"

"I don't care about your permits," the younger man said. "I'm not here to…"

Suddenly, the silence was broken about them. The howls erupted, and they were swarmed.

At least a half-dozen men, stretched and skeletal, gaunt from opiate and blood drinking, shrieked and ran towards them. Their skin was pale and scabbed, their clothing shreds of rusted nails and black leather tight against them. Their eyes were dark red from over use of Kryo, their cheeks sunken and grayed, their teeth sharpened to help them cut and devour the flesh of their victims. They were armed with crude weapons, hulks of metal and wood, shot through with nails and broken glass to create ugly mace-like bludgeons that they swung with speed and force towards the two men.

Then twin lights sliced through the darkness.

Laser blades.

Thin, blue lines, lancing through the curtain of night.

Wielded by the younger man with savagery and speed.

A deadly, silent ballet of death, slicing through the flesh and bone of the attackers, decimating them. With a few quicksilver moves from the younger man in the black coat, the pack was no more, now mere slabs of meat dripped to the ground, like their victims.

Within seconds, the streets were silent again.

And again, only two men stood.

One, breathing heavily, heart pounding like a machine gun, incredulous.

The other, standing next to him, in battle stance, eyes scanning over his victims in disgust, looking over the bodies of the newly slain, illuminated by the two light blue laser blades slashed from the silver and black steel scabbards clutched in his powerful hands.

The old man gathered his composure, still quaking, still unable to move his arms, stunned in disbelief over what he had just seen.

"Who… who… are you?" the old man said. "Are you Sikari? Vendari?"

The younger man's swords disappeared with a flash back into their scabbards.

He raised his hand to the skies and a jet black and silver hovercraft became uncloaked from its stealth mode. It lowered from the velvet curtain of the night, silently hovering before them, over the carnage.

The younger man gestured and the door of the vehicle opened. He motioned to the older man.

"Get in."

As the portal beckoned, a white light spilled forth, haloing both men, and for the first time, the old man could truly see the younger man before him.

Could see the cut of his face.

The jagged terrain of his gaze.

The color of his eyes.

Like earth and heaven at war, dark blood razing the earth at sun's fall.

Burned sienna.

Singed with gold.

The old man froze a moment, then knew he had no choice.

He walked tentatively towards the vehicle, climbing in, looking into the face of the man who held his life in his hands.

"Is it you, my friend? You look… different, but, it has been so many years since I last saw you, and, your eyes, is it, you?" the old man said. "The one who walks the earth, the man who will not die…"

The younger man took the wheel of the vehicle and sealed them in.

The old man's face turned from fear to wonder and then to fear again.

"You are him? The man I once knew? The man I once called my friend?" the old man said. "The Arimathean?"

"No," the younger man said. "I am not."

The older man instinctively twitched away.

"You… you are his son… Vanth the Destroyer," Xerxes said. "And you have come for me?"

"Yes," Vanth said.

"Is he… going to kill me? I . . . it was not me, not my fault. . . I didn't know. . . "

Xerxes voice trailed away and he shrunk into his seat.

"I thought . . . I tried . . ." he began, but stopped.

But Vanth the Destroyer remained silent, his eyes dark, his face stone, as the two men rose into the heavens, leaving the dead of the earth behind, quickly forgotten and left unmourned.

# FIVE

## Southwestern Iraq

## 1991

Something inside him knew there was a vast landscape out there, a world just outside his scope. But he could not make his way past the darkness and it frustrated him. So, he remained static, awaiting his fate.

By daylight, irregular waves of earth and rock touched the sky as far as Dorin Xerxes could see. But at night, especially now, the void was intimidating. The crescent moon offered little illumination and the pinpricks of stars next to nothing. He could make out the outlines of mountains, perhaps, a bit darker than the sky. A few yards of dirt and grass in front of him were bathed in the circular halo of his lantern, perched on a rock just outside the cave entrance. He went on sound as much he could, but the vagaries could be disorienting.

The click of Scorpio's machine gun against his artillery belt signaled the lieutenant's return. The dim glow of a beaten flashlight jiggled in the air as he advanced over unsteady ground.

Coming into Xerxes' sight, Scorpio shook his head, shrugged his shoulders, and blamed the thick curtain of blackness for his futility. He had found nothing out of the ordinary in his limited travels.

Xerxes sighed. Their desire to remain unseen ironically crippled their ability to see. And so, whatever it was that had flashed across the sky was bound to remain a mystery until daybreak.

The unknown tightened their nerves even more. Neither figured he would sleep tonight.

Xerxes thought of contacting base, but communications were to be kept to a minimum, left for absolute emergencies. Anything they sent out could and probably would be triangulated and would lead to them being discovered. They had been on the move since obtaining the object, taking it with the same force it would be assumed others would try to take it from them, if not more, once word of its discovery had gotten out.

They had monitored every aspect of the slow discovery, as had the other units around the planet. When they found it had been uncovered, they had no time to wait for backup. They moved in quickly, unexpectedly, while those who had pulled it from the ground were still celebrating obtaining it. They hit hard, with a full 21-man cadre of the Silent Hand, and by catching them off balance, Xerxes and his crew had been able to overcome them quickly and make away with the cargo. They made a short transmission to base and then changed channels and locations every few hours until settling in this remote outpost late in the evening, to remain here until they could be picked up and they and the cargo could be taken to a far more secure spot.

He wished they had had more soldiers.

But he understood the decision.

A cadre of more than 21 would arouse too much suspicion. And an army would certainly be easily spotted. The eyes of the enemy were everywhere. Many different factions had been searching for the object and any one of them could have found it, especially once they had narrowed down its location to this area.

Of the original nine, only seven remained.

The other two . . .

He wondered if he would suffer the same fate, as those others, those other innocents who had been slain "for the cause," as he had been told.

That wasn't what he had been told. This time.

He thought again about his decision, hoped it was the right one.

The country had been crawling with operatives from the different factions of which he was aware, and he was certain it had probably been home to some of which even he was not aware. All of them had been searching in this area of the world for more than a decade. A trail of bodies had led to this point. Xerxes hoped that theirs wouldn't be more added to the string of skulls.

He thought again of calling base.

No. If they hadn't found them by now, a call would allow the enemy to easily find them.

If it had been anything to fear, he would have recognized it.

He hoped.

The enemy was too cunning and at every point in the past, the all-seeing eye had seemed to arise from nowhere, as if it had been hiding in plain sight all along.

After they had finally secured it, his group had managed to keep the merchandise in secret, but he knew it wouldn't last. Its discovery began a clock, counting down to its next destination.

After a few short, fruitless moments of attempting to hear anything aside from the sound of insects, Scorpio descended into the cave to join the others, leaving Xerxes to the blind, ominous soundscape.

Maybe it had been nothing, he reassured himself. Just a falling star, a ball of rock and ice from somewhere light years away, meeting its end, betrayed by its own velocity, shearing against the force of the atmosphere.

Xerxes remembered a time not too long ago when he and his wife had seen a similar thing. Walking alone in the field beyond their home, they saw a streak of light breaking the serene sky. Basha was unsettled. He had to laugh. Her superstitions gave her more fear than the more pragmatic concern that it had been a missile or plane, about to exact a more certain doom than any archaic curse.

During their walks, the comets became a regular sight, a welcome complement to the inky darkness. They lent an air of the mystical to conversations heavy with too much life, too much death. At one point, she wondered how many others saw those same stars, in their spectacular death-throes, and then she was silent. And he knew she was wishing they could be anywhere but here.

Months later, in the midst of sobs, he would laugh again, wondering with dark humor if she had attached any promising omen to the last bright light falling from the sky that she saw. The one that would take her life, and the lives of their children, and herald a deluge that would needlessly destroy their town.

He had lived long, far longer than he ever imagined as a young man. But then he had no idea of the forces or technology he would encounter as he grew older, as he rose in rank through the secret society of warriors, the Silent Hand. Although close to a century old now, he was in better condition and health than most of the men around him who were decades younger.

But, as he had been told, by one who had lived far longer, that was both blessing and curse.

As he found in all too often burying loved ones.

What he had seen tonight was nothing like any projectile he had seen --- man-made, heaven-made or otherwise. It took improbable angles at impossible speeds, before coming to an abrupt halt and disappearing into thin air.

It could have just been a meteor, taking a violent path before disintegration. But it also could have been something unexpected and sinister. And so, as he slunk wearily to the ground, resting his back against a huge stone near the brush, his instinct for survival kept him from slipping away into sleep.

He thought once again of calling base. Cradling the communicator in his hand, resting his thumb against the switch, he clicked on it, only to find . . . silence.

Not even static.

He clicked on it again.

Silence.

The battery wasn't out. It wasn't malfunctioning earlier today.

He tried again.

Again, silence.

What was that?

Out of the corner of his eye, he could've sworn he had seen it.

His heart began to pound. His eyes darted across the sky.

This time, it was unmistakable. For just a few seconds, something, a shadow, eclipsing the moon.

There was no sound. He could hear no plane, no parachutes catching the wind.

Leaping to his feet, he quietly called to the others. Looking back up, he saw, again, something eclipsing the tail of the moon. More frantic now, he ordered them to the mouth of the cave, gesturing madly.

They scampered over broken rocks and makeshift paths, the clicking of automatic weapons to the ready echoing across the cavern walls, until the full squad of twenty-one were above ground at the ready.

A quick look over Xerxes' shoulder and he saw the first: A figure that looked like a man, descending slowly from the heavens, followed closely by another. He pointed his gun at the figures and strafed the sky as his soldiers followed suit.

For several minutes, the sounds of gunfire rattled over the landscape, explosions of light splattering the night sky, violent smacks of white fire against an impenetrable ebony canvas.

And then…nothing.

The sounds of insects and complete darkness.

Xerxes had seen at least two, Scorpio four. Others six, maybe seven. None could be sure. Xerxes sent them into the fields, weapons at the fore, flashlights guiding their sites, with instructions to shoot at anything breaking the path of their beams.

Quickly, Xerxes grabbed the radio and clicked it on. Static. A call to base. No answer. Again. No answer. He flicked around the channels, all the same. Static. Dead air.

It was then he heard the first scream.

A cacophony of gunfire and howls of pain. Bodies hitting the ground. Flashlights shattering.

And then…nothing.

Silence. Darkness.

Frantically, he clicked around the radio, searching in vain for anything, any sign of response. His gun and flashlight balanced in his other hand, before sweat slickened the metal and the light slithered from his grasp, hitting the ground hard, knocking the beam off, leaving him blind, alone, hands skittering over rocks and sand looking for the flashlight. He heard something, in front of him, advancing slowly.

"Scorpio? Who is that? Reply with the code or I'll fire!"

Silence.

He began firing wildly towards the noise, the machine gun fire drowning out a loud static suddenly emanating from the radio attached to his belt, drowning out his angry, powerless yelling, until a quick clicking announced an empty clip.

And the static died once more.

Silence.

A step forward and he heard the clink of hollow metal against his shoe. Ducking down, he lunged and his hand closed around the flashlight. A shake and the light clicked on in front of him.

Illuminating what he had been shooting at.

He gasped and fell backward.

There, not 10 feet in front of him, were seven men, or what looked like men. Tall, lanky, clad head to toe in a material that shimmered silver, black and gray, but strangely seemed to devour any light shined directly upon them. Their heads, or helmets --- he couldn't quite tell --- were slightly larger than normal. Small slits were barely raised above where their noses and mouths would be and dominating the faces were huge pairs of almond-shaped eyes that reflected like a cat's. Upon their chests and shoulders were red insignias, and symbols he recognized all too well.

Swastikas.

And even more astonishing was what floated around them like satellites: Bullets, scattered in massive clumps and at odd angles, suspended in mid-air, inches from the suits.

The figure at the fore lifted its arm and the gun yanked from Xerxes' hand and flew into the being's grasp. With an easy, almost casual strength, the being crushed the weapon into a crumpled mess.

From behind the figures, four of the Silent Hand emerged from the brush, savage and quick, swords at the ready, slicing a deadly path towards the figures. But it was for naught. The figures were able to deflect the blades without even touching them, pushing them away with what appeared to be magnetic fields, which were nevertheless disrupted as the swords crashed against them.

As the field crackled with light and dissonant sound, the radio came to life. Xerxes began yelling a distress call.

But with lightning speed, one of the beings snapped its fingers again and the radio emitted a shrill whine that caused Xerxes to drop it.

Somehow, with the being occupied with Xerxes' radio, Scorpio had managed to penetrate its force field and with a mighty swing of a sacred blade, he shattered the being's helmet and the body crumpled to the ground. However, that only served to enflame the others, as they savagely retaliated against the men, not only subduing them, but stealing their own swords from them and using the blades to cut them to pieces as they shrieked in the barren field.

Xerxes stood at the cave's mouth and pulled his own sword from its scabbard, but in one motion it was yanked from his grasp and flew into the hands of one of the beings. With another wave of the being's hand, Xerxes was shoved by an invisible force against the cave's mouth, his back smacking hard against the stone. He fell to the ground in pain, but reached down to grab twin daggers from his boots and rise once more. But as if annoyed more than threatened, the being merely raised its hand and shoved Xerxes back with unseen force against the rock, forcing him to drop the blades and leaving Xerxes fallen in pain.

He moved backwards toward the cave, his light still fixed on the beings, when he felt a cold inside his chest and he was paralyzed, unable to move, frozen, holding the light aloft, enabling him to see his men being cut down in front of him.

His heart flew and he raced to finish prayers as rapidly as he could remember them, figuring he was seconds from death, unable to do anything but watch as the beings slowly walked toward him.

Four of them strode into the cave.

One left behind knelt and turned its head, seemingly examining Xerxes. Looking into its eyes, he felt a fear deeper than any that had haunted him in the past. But despite his imagination leading in gruesome directions, the being did nothing. It seemed content to merely observe him.

Minutes later, the other figures emerged from the cave, with the large wooden box housing the merchandise, perched upon what looked like a stainless steel sled. The sled and box hovered about a foot above the ground, rising or slowly turning to avoid anything blocking its path.

Once outside the cave, several yards into the field stretching out before them, the figures stopped and surrounded their cargo, and above them, a glowing saucer appeared, slowly levitating down.

Xerxes swallowed hard as the being towered over him. Raising its hand, it motioned upward and Xerxes, still locked into the same position, rose from the ground, hovering a few feet above the hard ground below. Oddly, he felt a warm sensation fill his body, and his limbs relaxed as he was stood upright, still limp, and unable to move. But what was most unusual was that his desire to move had completely disappeared.

It was then the piercing filled his head, the pain, excruciating, pounding, stabbing, increasing as he struggled against it, against the invasion, and he felt the blood begin to pool and burst and drip from his ears.

He prepared himself to die, his life flashing before him, but just as his vision began to blur, he saw the figure emerging from the dark expanse, the familiar shade of a man he had known years before.

The Arimathean.

With a savage swing of the Arimathean's fiery indigo holy blade, the black figure torturing Xerxes was sent writhing to the ground in agony, seemingly crying out to its compatriots. It tried to rise, tried to fight back, but there was no defense as the Arimathean drove the sacred flame of Soulsfire through the heart of the being and its blood drained into the rock and dirt.

At the sight of their dark brethren felled, the other figures frantically gestured and a beam of light flashed down from the saucer, enveloping them and the box. Slowly, they began to rise upward into an oval portal that had opened in the craft.

The Arimathean wasted no time, hurtling himself towards the light and into it. With a flash, he ignited Soulsfire, and it erupted in a fang of blue flame. A burst of white light and red lightning crackled about the beam of light, shutting down the lumen transportation column from the craft and dropping the box and the beings to the ground, along with the Arimathean.

He landed like a cat, quick, on his feet, and before the beings could recover, he was upon them, slashing at the dark figures with the indigo blade of the holy sword, ripping through their armor and sending them collapsing to the ground as a black ooze emitted from their dying bodies.

A thinner beam of light flashed down from the saucer, enveloping only the wooden box, and again the box began to rise, quicker than before. But the Arimathean whipped the holy sword towards the light beam, disrupting it again, and the wooden vessel dropped once more to the ground with a thick thud.

The two remaining figures alive took advantage of the distraction to attack the Arimathean furiously, but with equal ferocity and speed, the Arimathean pulled two steel fangs of death, his samurai swords, from their scabbards. Forged in the black mountains of Tibet just beyond the Golden City, they were indestructible and possessed of the power of the two Annunaki stones which lay embedded in their thick, silver and black handles. The force fields of the beings offered no resistance. With a grotesque and blindingly fast pattern of destruction, the blades laid waste to the two remaining figures, decapitating one and slicing the other in two.

Once more, the beam flashed down upon the box, but again, the Arimathean leapt into it, grabbing onto the box tightly. It lurched and tilted, a struggle between heavens and earth, as the immortal warrior clung to it.

From the corners of the craft, two red lasers shot towards the Arimathean, bathing the beam in red light and incredible heat, causing his skin to sweat and blister. He cried out in pain, but remained clinging to the box, barely.

His body wracked in agony and covered in sweat, his grip slickened and even with his nails and grasp dug into the box he began to falter, slowly, as the lasers were joined by two others, increasing the intensity of the heat within the beam and causing the wooden box to begin to smolder and burst into flame. The Arimathean's grasp faltered as the wood blackened and crumbled in his hands.

With one last burst of flame turning the wood to char, the box cracked and crumbled away to reveal a massive, glimmering golden sarcophagus ripe with precious jewels and baroque mystic symbols. The Arimathean attempted to grab ahold of the golden object, but to no avail. The craft shot violently upward and the Arimathean was shoved from the beam and plummeted to the earth, landing hard against the tough ground as the craft pulled the object into it and hurtled into the sky at an ever quicker pace until disappearing into the clouds.

The Arimathean lay on the dirt, wounded, not far from where Xerxes also laid on the hard rock, bleeding and tormented by incredible pain.

The Arimathean rose with a groan and looked around quickly, scanned for any other threats, found none, then approached Xerxes, put his hand under his head and gave him water.

"Are you alright?" the Arimathean said.

"As much as possible," Xerxes said. "Are any of the others?"

The Arimathean shook his head.

"So much death . . . " Xerxes said. "Too much. For too long. Always fighting the same battles. Over the same . . . for centuries . . ."

"Longer than that," the Arimathean said, his face growing dark, as he looked to Xerxes' wounds.

"You're going to be alright, someone will be here soon," the Arimathean said.

"But for what purpose?" Xerxes gasped.

The Arimathean looked at him cryptically.

The radio began to kick in and a voice scratched over it. The Arimathean handed it to Xerxes.

"You take care of this."

"Not now," Xerxes said, ignoring it, and struggling to his feet, standing, barely. "There is nothing good to say."

The Arimathean strode over to the dark, fallen figures.

"They don't have much to say either," he said, as he knelt above one of the dead who had attacked them, holding a light in one hand to illuminate the fallen as his other went to the helmet of the being. "Now let's see who they . . ."

With one motion of incredible strength, the Arimathean ripped the helmet off the figure he had just killed, and for a second, even he was stunned, as the face was revealed in the beam of the flashlight. Then Xerxes saw as well, the face, and went silent, as the voices on the radio called out for response, but he could give none. He was in shock.

They looked at each other, then down at the face of the fallen being.

Then the Arimathean, driven by a churning in his gut, strode over and grabbed another being that had been killed, pulled its body towards them, and once again, ripped off what remained of its helmet from Scorpio's blow.

He flashed the light at the dead being's face.

And again, he recoiled.

"It is him, or a replica of him," Xerxes said. "But . . . how?"

And there before them, there before the immortal warrior and the man who had stood by his side now and decades before, were two bodies. Dead. Pale.

And each with the same face.

The same identical face.

The face of the man they had killed so many years before.

The face of the man who had killed so many thousands of others, who had poisoned their world.

Dead. By their own hands.

But . . . somehow . . . alive, in both beings, identical in all ways to the man they had killed.

The throne of evil.

Adolf Hitler.

Their stunned numbness was broken by a thunderous boom from above.

The craft.

It had been joined by a second.

High above them, the two craft glowed, locked in what appeared to be a firefight, red lightning ripping from each to envelop the other, holding them conjoined in a tug of war that tore the sky with light and violent fury.

Xerxes snapped to, caught a snippet from the radio being transmitted to them over and over.

"Capulet!"

Shock and urgency gripped both of their faces.

"The cave!" The Arimathean called out, grabbing Xerxes, and slinging him over his shoulders, carrying him down into the cavern and moving as quickly as he could down, down, far into the earth, as far as possible from the surface and the battle above.

"Do you think?" Xerxes said.

"They have before," the Arimathean replied, continuing to move as fast as he could with the injured body of his friend. "Twice."

And then a flash came from the opening above, penetrating even deep into the cave, and the earth rocked with incredible force, causing stones to dislodge from the ceiling, but the Arimathean continued on, ever more quickly.

And then, a second explosion from above and the force sent the two of them forward, down into the underground room haloed in steel that they had used as base, had used to shield the merchandise.

With merely a thought and a glance at the control panel, the Arimathean shut the reinforced steel doors behind them, sealing them in, and they listened as two more explosions ripped the earth above.

And then, silence.

# SIX

## Southeastern airspace outside Dallas

## November 1963

He walked to his seat on the plane, exhausted, confused.

And there, placed neatly, it sat.

Upon seeing it, he instinctively recoiled from it, startled.

He looked around, glanced quickly, to see if anyone was watching him, looking to see his reaction, but no eyes caught his, none needed to. The object's presence was enough.

There on his seat.

One black rose.

His heart pounded in his chest.

He could feel the sweat drip down his neck, down his back.

With a flick of a magazine, he swatted it off, then kicked it beneath the chair in front of him.

But its message was clear.

Unless he wanted to find himself in the same position as his predecessor, he knew what he had to do.

And that was, quite simply, whatever they told him to do.

# SEVEN

## Washington, D.C.

## March 1981

As he felt his life slipping away, felt himself losing his grip, his chest welled up with blood and fear, and he grasped, grasped at the last precipice, and surrendered.

"He's saying something!"

The doctor leaned in, to hear the dying man's whisper.

"Black... pearl..."

With the confusion of distraction, no one noticed.

No one noticed, that the second doctor had leaned in, leaned in towards the dying man, and placed a gloved hand, one hiding a tiny syringe, beneath the old man's opposite arm, and injected him with the contents.

The first doctor, taking the cue, went through the motions, and acted relieved and astounded when a strengthening beep began to emerge upon the medical instruments.

"He's... alive... he's... coming back..." the doctor said. "He's recovering. I think he's going to be ok."

And the old man looked up, as the light began to flood back into his eyes, the life back into his body, and while his heart filled with relief, it was a bittersweet flood.

And his eyes opened again, his mind realized what had happened, and his eyes began to well, glaze over, with tears he could not cry.

# EIGHT

**Goddard Space Center**

**Greenbelt, Maryland**

**April 22, 2010**

**4 a.m.**

The two men emerged from the elevator, greeted by the third. They strode briskly down the hall, the director, short and bespectacled, still groggy from having been woken, disheveled in loose fitting jeans, white shirt, and black tie; the scientist, paunchy and rumpled in khakis, white shirt, and blue tie, amped and jumpy from what he knew; and the third, calmly gliding towards the room he knew well, immaculately dressed in dark suit and deep violet tie, white shirt, taut, tanned and handsome, with close cropped hair peppered with gray.

"I'm sorry, I wouldn't have disturbed you if it wasn't . . .
" the scientist began.

The director dismissed the apology with a wave of his
hand.

"Obviously if you couldn't tell me over the phone, it is,"
the director replied. "So, what is it?"

"I'd still rather wait until we can get to command to
show you," the technician said, as they hurried their pace.

The director looked to the man in black.

The man in black nodded. "We've been monitoring the
situation," the man said, coldly.

Once in the clandestine command center, a trio of
massive steel doors sealed shut behind them. Before them were a
long string of desks dotted with a sprawling number of buttons
and instruments, many of which were blinking frantically. Above
them were several herculean video screens taking up most of the
far wall.

There were several levels of NASA. Each represented a
level of knowledge allowed. At the bottom of the pyramid was
what the public, and the largest number of scientists, were
allowed to see, after the information received had been filtered
down through the lines. The newscasts showing dozens of
scientists in a large room filled with arcane technology were
nothing more than a façade. One that covered what those truly in

charge of NASA had known since its inception, and which, in fact, fueled its inception.

The room the three men were in was at the top of the pyramid, and as such only five other scientists, with the highest security clearance, were allowed in it.

And even they had no idea of the other levels, beyond the pyramid.

Those represented by the man in black.

Frank Case.

The director of a top secret international agency that had been in existence for centuries, founded to deal with threats and beings other agencies weren't equipped to handle.

Capulet.

"Something has reprogrammed Voyager 2," the scientist said. "We lost control of it shortly after midnight, and a few minutes later, we started getting this data."

He showed them a skein of odd symbols and sigils that had been printing off and several screens working to decipher them. We've recorded it all and run it through cryptology but haven't come up with anything yet.

Case looked at the paper.

The director looked at Case.

"Any ideas?" the director asked.

"Possibly," Case said.

The director had seen that look in Case's eyes before. More than a few times. Particularly in the past two decades.

"Sub rosa," Case said to the scientist, who nodded energetically in response. Case raised his arm and a hologram appeared above it. He manipulated a few of the images and dotted the symbols. "I'll have two men here within the hour. We'll remain a presence until further notice."

The scientist nodded.

"If anyone asks, this was a software problem with the flight data system," Case said. "We'll handle disinfo."

The director and the scientist agreed.

"No one enters or leaves this room without Capulet approval," Case said.

The scientist nodded in agreement and held out his hand. Case took it.

"Thank you," the scientist said.

"Thank you," Case replied with a slight smile.

Case and the director left the room.

Case looked hard at the director.

"You know what I'm going to ask," Case said.

The director nodded.

"Two."

Case nodded.

"Courier," Case said. "We'll take care of it."

The elevator opened. The director shook Case's hand.

"They're good men," the director said. "Good men."

Case nodded. "Sometimes that's why," Case said.

"They have families, children," the director said. "Please. I know what you have to do. But . . . they've gotten to this point and there have been no reports."

"Understood," Case said. "Ultra will take care of it. You'll be notified. They'll need to be reassigned."

The director felt relieved. "Thank you."

Case nodded.

"Is this connected to the others?" the director asked.

"Probably," Case said. "You've been monitoring the Knight; Luna; you know they've been receiving."

"And sending," the director said.

"Yes," Case said.

"Thule?" the director asked.

Case shook his head slightly.

"Vendari?"

"Possibly."

"Could it be benign? Sikari? Silent Hand?"

"None of them are completely benign," Case said. "That's why we exist."

# NINE

## Geneva, Switzerland

## August 5, 1945

The Columbia was perched within the penthouse, looming above the city. The restaurant was a glistening edifice, a daunting symbol of elitism and inaccessibility. But never more so than on this evening, when only three people were seated at an elaborate table in the middle of its vast expanse, the building otherwise closed off to the public.

Closed by its owner.

The man seated at the head of the table.

He didn't bother with introductions. They knew who he was. He knew who they were. That was why they were here.

The man was elegantly and immaculately clothed in a fine navy pinstripe wool suit, with white Egyptian cotton shirt and a crimson and gold silk tie. His hair was long and blonde, pulled back from his Nordic features and piercing steel-blue eyes. He was of indeterminate age. He looked and carried himself as an older man, calm and imposing, but he looked much younger.

A second, larger, muscular man of similarly pale countenance, wearing a similar suit, stood silently to the side of the table, a few yards back from it.

Dorin Xerxes sat to the right of the Nordic. The Arimathean to his left.

Upon the table were an array of elaborate trays, each decorated with exotic and delicious dishes, alongside a line of beverages of ancient vintage.

"How is your meal?" the Nordic asked.

"It is… extraordinary," Xerxes said. "But I would expect no less."

"Nor would I present you with any less," the Nordic said.

"Thank you."

The Arimathean remained silent, as he had throughout the meal.

"I am… very sorry, very sorry for your loss," the Nordic said, gazing intently at the Arimathean. "I wish I, I wish we, could have helped."

Xerxes looked at the Arimathean with sympathy and curiosity. They had shared many battles together throughout the war, but he knew very little about him. He knew of the eternal's power only through legend. He had heard he could not die. And he knew, he had seen, that he could not be permanently wounded for it would heal, however miraculously. That he had the power to transcend the worlds, briefly travel between dimensions, but could not escape this one.

But now, he was just a man, a crumpled and sad hollow of a human being, who had just lost someone he loved dearly. His daughter. Cancer. It had been discovered and advanced rapidly. Within six weeks of seeing the doctor for what seemed a routine cough, she was gone. Just like her mother, not even a year before.

And yet another part of him had died as well, another chip from a rock that had crumbled greatly over the course of more than two millennia.

He had gone to fight to keep the world safe for her, for her future.

And now she had no future. And he, once more, was uncertain of anything for his own, other than pain, suffering and, as always, conflict.

Xerxes looked softly at him.

"I am sorry, my friend."

The Arimathean's body slumped, his face grown cold and dark.

The Nordic placed his utensils onto his plate, looked to the two men and sighed.

"I respect you too much to adhere to any further pretense, and don't wish to make this experience any more uncomfortable or unpleasant," the Nordic said. "You know why you are here. You know what I would like from you. And you know what I am prepared to offer you."

The Nordic looked to the Arimathean, then to Xerxes.

"Exactly what we have spoken about, not so far in the past," the Nordic said.

Xerxes' face feigned disbelief, ignorance, but betrayed fear.

"I don't…"

"Please, my friend," the Nordic said, cordially. "You know I know everything."

Xerxes' face grew pale.

"Your role in the inner circle is quite clear," the Nordic said to Xerxes. "You are one of the only men who have knowledge of the whereabouts of, and have access to, many of the artifacts the Nazis themselves had obtained. And two of those articles you hold are two which I, and my family, once held, which I had acquired over the lifeless bodies of many men before you, with far less cordiality and negotiation."

"I...I..." Xerxes said, barely above a rasp.

"Please do not lie to me and waste both our time," the Nordic said. "You know my father. You know I am here representing him. He is a civil man. I am a civil man, and I do honor you and our friendship with your order. I hope we can easily come to an amicable agreement so we can continue to enjoy the evening. I don't ask for any of the artifacts other than the two which once belonged to me and my bloodline, which belong to the Vendari."

"What makes you think I would know where they are?" Xerxes said.

The Nordic smiled and lightly shook his head in disbelief.

"You know far more than you say, it is typical of the Silent Hand, but particularly of you, in your position in the order," the Nordic said.

He nodded towards the Arimathean.

"I know you brought him with you anticipating this," the Nordic said. "Anticipating a battle which does not need to occur. There's no reason for it. We're not asking for anything but the recovery of what the Thule had taken from us, and which you took from the Thule. I know you are not telling me everything, and that is not required. Words are meaningless without action. Say what you will, or do not, we merely request the return of what is rightfully ours."

The Nordic looked again towards the Arimathean.

"You haven't even told him everything, your order has merely been using him in this conflict, knowing he would grasp the magnitude of it and leave his seclusion to help you," the Nordic said, looking the Arimathean in the eyes. "You are being lied to. They have been pursuing the same artifacts, the same sarcophagi, we all have, and they mean to use it the same as we all do."

"Why are you telling me this?" the Arimathean said.

"Because we respect you. And because it's the truth. You are wasting your life and your time on this planet with these . . . primitive, parochial conflicts. And you know it."

The Arimathean remained silent.

The Nordic turned again to Xerxes.

"I can offer you wealth and luxury beyond your imagination," the Nordic said to him. "I can offer you decades longer of existence through science you and the rest of humanity are completely unaware of."

He looked at the Arimathean.

"Or which is being kept from you," the Nordic said, sardonically.

Xerxes thought for a moment, considered what he was being offered, what he was being told, but he quickly stopped himself, chastised himself for considering it, and a rage slowly began to rise within him.

"You are a liar," Xerxes said. "Like the demon you represent."

The Nordic sighed.

"You call him a demon, I call him Dad," the Nordic said.

"You certainly have his sense of humor," the Arimathean said.

"There are no demons, no angels," the Nordic said. "That is nothing but a human way of explaining beings beyond their world and beyond their comprehension. Beings that, like you, are good and evil, only more powerful. Power is neutral. It is only in how it is used that we can ascribe any sort of moral value to it. We are not demons. Nor angels. We are nothing but creations of the universe, of what you call God, like you, only millennia beyond you on the evolutionary scale and the dimensional wavelength. You would think by now your overlords in the Silent Hand would've told you that, at least, instead of allowing you to wallow in your primitive ignorance."

"Spoken like a descendant of Lucifer, a prince of lies," Xerxes said.

"You know he hates that name," the Nordic said, rolling his eyes. "But you humans never seem to tire of it. You would think you could've come up with something more creative over three or four millennia, but, apparently not."

The Nordic sighed again, sitting back in his chair.

"I have the power to kill you, if I so wanted. You know this. But I am still an honorable man. I want to give you the choice. The decision."

"There is no decision to be made," Xerxes said.

"So I see," the Nordic said. "But, in that decision, it appears you will have a decision after all."

He handed Xerxes an odd, oblong golden pill.

"It will be quick and painless. I promise you a sacred burial, in accordance with your wishes, with your traditions."

Xerxes threw the pill in the face of the Nordic.

"When you die," Xerxes said, "when you finally die, I hope you rot in hell."

The pill fell to the floor and rolled into the corner.

"But I know you will," Xerxes said to the Nordic, finally addressing him by name, "Azazel."

The second man who had been standing, unmoved, retrieved the pill.

Held it up to Azazel, who took it from him.

"Thank you, Baruchel," Azazel said.

Azazel, annoyed, shook his head slowly.

"There is no rotting, there is no hell, only lower dimensions and higher, which you ascend or descend depending on the energy you accumulate on the plane from which you depart," Azazel said, putting the pill into his coat pocket and once more sighing. "I grow tired of this."

Azazel looked at his watch.

"What are you doing?" Xerxes said.

The Arimathean stared at the men, coldly.

"What are you…"

Xerxes began to choke, began clutching his throat with one hand, his other outstretched to the Arimathean, then, slapped onto the table to hold him up.

"Poison…" Xerxes gasped.

With a flash, the Arimathean grasped his sword, but even as his hand closed around the scabbard of the sacred blade, Soulsfire, he felt himself caught in a torrent of lightning that exploded from the table near him and swirled around him like an electric cocoon, holding him frozen and barely able to move, despite his struggle.

Azazel looked at the Arimathean and smirked.

"Are you surprised?" Azazel said. "You didn't think I would prepare for you? You didn't think that we, the Vendari, would have access to a Centauri stone?"

The Nordic walked slowly around the table, around Xerxes continuing to grasp his neck, struggling for breath, and the Arimathean, static but battling within the sorcerous prison of lightning rippling about him, increasing in intensity the more he vainly fought to free himself.

"My apologies," Azazel said to the Arimathean. "I know I can't kill you, and honestly, we have no desire to even harm you. We respect you. But you stand in our way, so you need to be neutralized."

He looked at Xerxes, coughing and gagging as he writhed upon the table.

"You, on the other hand," the Nordic sighed, walking around him. "I am still an honorable man. I offered you the opportunity for a quick death, an honorable burial, after a long life. Instead you chose the alternative."

"What... what.... Did you...." Xerxes gasped.

"I did nothing I couldn't have done the moment you walked in," the Nordic sniffed condescendingly. "Poison. How vulgar for you to even consider me so crude. You act as if I don't have the power to crush your windpipe slowly with merely a thought, merely a minor spell, the slightest use of Vendari magicks."

Azazel held up the pill.

"This pill honestly would have killed you almost instantly," he said. "I wasn't lying about that. I am a man of my word. But either way, your fate was sealed when you refused merely to return to us that which is ours. Now we'll only be forced to take it. Or, at least, at first, request it. I'll send the note to your masters in your coffin. Perhaps that will deliver the message with adequate force."

Xerxes gasped, then fell to the table, his eyes glazed but looking upward to the Arimathean, his ears still alive, hearing his every word.

"I'll . . . I'll . . ." Xerxes reached out for the pill.

The doors to the room burst open and three men clad in dark hazmat suits and masks and stylized sorceric armor emblazoned with Sanskrit sigils flew into the room, strange stainless steel weapons in hand, blasting blue pulses of light toward the two Vendari. The larger, muscular man, hit by two of the beams, was stopped cold as he reached for a weapon. His hands balled into fists as he tried running towards the men in the suits, but their weapons increased in power and the beams widened, turning a crimson red, charring the man's flesh as he fell to the ground dead.

Azazel didn't attempt to move. He remained caught in the blue pulse of the beam from the lead man in the suit who had led the other two through the door.

The lead man in the suit nodded to the other two and they trained their blue beams upon the Nordic, who merely smiled sardonically.

"Take him to Aviary," the lead man said in a metallic voice through the mask. One of the two others kept the blue beam upon the Nordic, while the second threw a small, round metallic device into the beam. It began to circle, slowly, around Azazel, containing the blue light in a halo around his body, leaving him imprisoned as the two men, guns still pointing at the Nordic, led him from the room.

The lead man strode over to Xerxes, who was still collapsed on the floor, gasping for air, and kneeled beside him, checking his throat. While the constraints upon his throat had loosened once Azazel was caught in the beam, he was still wracked by pain and struggling to breathe through his injured windpipe.

The lead man took off his mask, revealing his sharp features and close-cropped hair.

"Case," Xerxes gasped.

Frank Case looked him over. "You're going to be fine."

Case stood up and watched as the bolts around the Arimathean began to lessen in intensity as Azazel left the room, until finally the blue flame of Soulsfire erupted and with a boom and flash of light the electrical beams imprisoning him exploded and dissipated.

Immediately the Arimathean looked down, beneath the table, to find the Centauri stone, a silver oval carved with ancient amethyst runes which purred as he lifted it and placed it into a pocket on his belt.

"Souvenir?" Case quipped.

"Hard to come by," the Arimathean scowled. "Nephilim Elohim magick. Very rare. Never know when you might need it."

Case looked down as Xerxes sat up and Case helped him to rise to his feet.

"I didn't . . . tell him anything," Xerxes rasped.

"We know," Case said. "Capulet knows all."

"Were you monitoring this whole time?" the Arimathean asked.

Case nodded. "We wanted to see what he would reveal, what we would learn about which of the artifacts the Vendari may have found, or, obtained."

"How many of the thirteen have you found?" the Arimathean said, as Case seemed surprised for a moment at the number mentioned. "Not counting the spear we recovered or the others."

"We've located two of the sarcophagi," Case said.

"Where?" Xerxes said. "We need to . . . ."

Case raised his hand, palm up, slightly, to calm him.

"Japan," Case said, as he walked away from the men, looking out towards the window. "Two different locations."

Case's countenance grew stern and he looked out the window upon the city.

"Don't worry," Case said. "We have the situation under control."

"Those words have been spoken countless times," the Arimathean said. "And rarely have they resembled truth."

# TEN

## Rural upstate New York

## 2042

Outside of the city, the sky opened to a panorama of stars and fields of darkness broken by the lily pads of light that made up the free-range zones.

Once the cities had become diseased, those with means or ingenuity fled to the country, engineering a new way. They created oases of their own, upon which they grew their own food and conducted their own lives apart from the masses. Some of them lived in domes, others in traditional farms and homes they had found and claimed after the brief civil wars, inherited or built themselves.

Some of them remained chipped, most of them removed the circuits, preferring to live off-grid.

All, whether they realized it or not, remained under surveillance by the satellites and drones which periodically patrolled their area, hidden under stealth cloaking, to keep an eye on them and to monitor any potential dissent or rebellion.

Or . . . any other suspicious or unusual activity.

Largely, they were left alone. They posed little threat and their ideologies stood little chance of penetrating the willful fog of ignorance and entertainment occupied by the vast majority of the populace.

After the secessions and the regional wars that followed in the remaining states, the power structure had overtly and covertly created control mechanisms to keep the population in line.

Those in the free-range zones, in many ways, had created their own control mechanisms. They willfully disengaged and had no interest in re-integrating. And so, those running the cities paid them little mind. They kept them under watch, but experience had shown little reason to be diligent, as most were pacifists and outcasts, with little interest in returning to the cities, let alone overthrowing them.

Zinesha had grown up among them.

Grown up as a girl named Zinesha.

After she had been brought to them as a girl named Natasha.

She had little memory of her time in the regular world, but remembered it, like here, was spent in the country.

Only somewhere far, far away, much colder than here.

Her father had died, she was told.

And her mother, as well, shortly after she arrived in the free-range zone, so far away, thousands of miles, over the ocean and land.

She was raised by an aunt, whose husband had long ago died and had never remarried. Who taught her how to live off the land. Who taught her to fight. Who taught her compassion. The compassion and love she had been missing since her parents had passed.

Her name had been changed when she moved here.

It was for her safety, they said.

She wasn't sure what they meant.

But she figured it had something to do with her father. And how he had disappeared. And how she last remembered him, softly padding into her room when she was half asleep, and brushing aside her hair, and kissing her forehead, telling her he loved her. Her eyes still closed, she smiled, and slightly opened one eye to see him slip from her room.

Heard the howls. The noises outside.

Listened as she heard the door to their home open. Heard him tell her mother he loved her.

And then heard him leave.

And that was the last she had heard him.

There were times, growing up, that she could've sworn she heard him.

Times when she woke up in the middle of the night, and could've sworn she heard her father's voice.

And then, in pieces, but occluded, as if behind an opaque screen, she would catch snippets of memory.

Of being woken in the middle of the night.

Of being taken away, along with her mother.

Of the man who had taken them. The man her mother said had helped them.

She remembered little about him.

Little but the sound of his voice.

His scent.

And his eyes.

So dark, distant, but with strange fire, a flame of gold.

She shivered.

Looked out through the window of the hovercraft, to the halos of light below.

"Where are we going?" Zinesha said.

"Somewhere safe," Bastian said. "For now, at least."

"For now?"

"No place is safe forever," Bastian said.

"But you're Sikari, you're descended from a Magi," Zinesha said. "What could harm you?"

"You don't want to know," Bastian said.

"Try me," Zinesha said. "I may as well know. You're bringing me with you for some reason."

Bastian smiled slightly.

"There's a war that's been going on for a while, that's about to erupt, and escalate," Bastian said.

"You mean like the civil wars?" Zinesha said.

"No," Bastian said, "those were engineered, to get people under control. This is . . . in no one's control."

"What do you mean?"

"This has been going on for millennia, for as long as humankind has been here," Bastian said. "But, if the signs and all the prophecies are correct, it may soon be coming to an end."

"And that's good, right?" Zinesha said.

"It depends," Bastian said.

"On what?"

"On who wins."

Bastian halted, her attention clasped, her heart frozen.

Just over the horizon, she could see the smoke, rising.

And as they grew closer, the flames, the wreckage, the remains.

Bastian looked down upon the carnage, the destruction, probably no more than an hour old, and the flames reflected in her dark violet eyes.

They knew.

And they too were coming for the girl.

And she, inadvertently, may have led the girl right into their trap.

"What happened?" Zinesha said, looking down at the burning remains, the fallen biodomes, the charred farmland, below them.

"Something that would've happened to us if we had gotten here earlier," Bastian said. "We have to go."

Bastian reached into a pouch on her belt, pulled a small crystal from it. She pressed a button on the dashboard of the craft and a tiny compartment opened. She popped the crystal in, then closed it. It began to glow and emitted a slight hum and the craft itself began to hum, louder and louder, and glow, brighter and brighter.

"Where are we going?" Zinesha said.

Bastian turned the vehicle around and veered it west.

She looked at Zinesha. "Away from here."

As her words hung in the air, their craft was rocked with blaster fire from three black, triangular Thule ships behind them.

"Damn it," Bastian said. "They knew we were coming here. Stupid. I should've known it would be a trap."

"Did they track us?" Zinesha said.

"No, I found and disabled the tracking device in here after we got on board," Bastian said. "They got here first and were waiting. The same as they were in the holo-bar. Which means someone is feeding them information and they're anticipating our moves."

"What are we going to do?" Zinesha said.

"What I always do," Bastian said. "Kick ass and ask questions later."

Her eyes slanted and her jaw grew tight as her face steeled with concentration. Her muscles flared as she pulled the steering wheel tight towards her and the craft made a swift maneuver upward and into a spiral, before diving downward, pulling up just before impact to level parallel with the ground.

Then she pulled back again and the craft zoomed upward at an obscene angle, behind the Thule craft that had been pursuing them.

"Take notes," Bastian smirked.

She unloaded a torrent of blaster fire upon the three black triangular craft that had been pursuing them, tearing into the manta-shaped fighters, and sending two of them hurtling to the ground. The third, however, was too nimble, and avoided fire. It spun agilely and returned fire at Bastian's craft, grazing it, igniting a torrent of sparks inside the craft.

"Dammit," Bastian said.

"What was that about kicking ass?" Zinesha said.

"Sometimes it takes more than one kick," Bastian said, as she engaged in a deadly ballet with the Thule craft, as they zipped and zagged through the air around each other, waiting to line up a kill shot.

The Thule fighter ripped off a blast that careened off the back of the hovercraft, sending it into a spin, hurtling towards the ground. Looking for the coup de gras, the ebon triad shot downward towards Bastian's hovercraft, firing wildly in an attempt to strike.

But much to the surprise of the Thule, she halted the spiral, pulled up on the brake and sent the hovercraft ripping upward, past and over the Thule craft, and as she did, she opened fire, sending bright red beams cutting into the cartilage of her enemy's fighter.

The Thule craft vomited flame and smoke as it slowly sputtered downward, its pilot attempting to keep it from crashing.

"Hold on," Bastian said.

She sent their craft into a spiral downwards after the Thule craft, continuing to land blast shots upon it, and as it crashed, they landed a short distance from it. Bastian quickly unbuckled herself, pushed the button to open the hatch, pulled her sword and blaster, and turned to Zinesha.

"You stay here!"

"But . . ."

"But nothing! Stay!"

"What do I do next, roll over?" Zinesha crossed her arms and slunk back in her seat.

Bastian leapt from the craft, sprinting towards the fallen Thule craft while keeping her blade up in defensive position, waiting for the pulse of a blaster to shriek towards her. But it never came. She got to the craft and it was a smoldering mess, its pilot dead, half flung from the cockpit in a vain attempt to eject before impact.

She stood over his prone body, her blaster at his face, at the ready at the slightest sign of him moving, but none came. Her hand reached out and, as her father had taught her, she breathed deeply and let her astral form penetrate the residual electrical field of the fallen Thule, into his brain, absorbing the synapses and letting her instantly process them per magnetic code, reading his mind, or what was left of it, until she could connect with the correct neural pathways she wanted, ripping forth from his brain the information she needed.

Whether she wanted to know it, or not.

A torrent of images flooded her brain, until a few spiked and exploded, jolting her to action.

She pulled away from the warrior and stood up. She ran back to the hovercraft and bolted inside, buckled up.

"We have to go, now," Bastian said.

"Away from here again?" Zinesha said.

"No," Bastian said, "this time I know exactly where we need to go, and I pray we get there, before it's too late."

# ELEVEN

## Sedona, Arizona

## 2042

Below a rust red rocky outcropping, beneath a golden desert, a triangular edifice of crystal and amethyst was alive, completely obscured by the barren land above.

It was one of many such compounds of this sort, all acting as dwelling places and command centers near the perimeter of New California. All of them helmed by a quasi-secret society that had been founded over a thousand years prior.

The Order of the Sikari.

A week earlier, an ornate box had been delivered to this place, and since then, a sense of dread had permeated the Sikari edifice, even here, in this space of sacred spires constructed upon vibrant ley lines.

The Oculus Box was a slightly rectangular object, no more than a foot across, a little less than that deep, with gold and onyx hieroglyphs spread across it like a sinister web, veins of apocalyptic visions bled out from the dark figure drawn in the center, which had, embedded in where it's heart would be, a single gem. Milky white and shimmering with prisms and dark stars as the light hit it. An oculus stone. It had traveled across the world after its recent discovery, never remaining in one place for too long, to keep it out of the hands of those who would use the object inside of it for nefarious means.

Its power was incredible, and with it carried an aura of malice and dread.

Within seconds of its arrival, the headaches and nausea began to seep over some of the women, those who were more recent recruits to the holy order of warriors and hadn't ascended to the levels necessary to fully block psychic attack.

They had no idea what was in the box. Only the highest of their order did. They initially talked as if it might have been a radioactive or biological toxin. But that wouldn't explain the shrieks in their ears, and even more disconcerting, in their heads.

The day had been filled with a palpable foreboding. Radar within the complex and electromagnetic, visual, and thermal scanners outside had registered little out of the ordinary, aside from some slight, aberrant energy readings. But Judeai, the general of the complex, could not shake a sense of impending danger.

These were holy warriors. Paladins of the Delphic Order. Women who had followed the One of the Cave, the one bearing the scars, the last of the bloodline of Patmos.

Trained at the foot of Novus Spiritus. The bloodline of the Revelator.

Only they could be entrusted to guard an artifact of such power, which could crush the minds of ordinary humans like robins' eggs.

It had been hidden, here, underneath a sacred spire, to bind the demonic power inside, as it remained surrounded constantly by a revolving cadre of priests chanting to preserve its metaphysical prison, as it thrashed about within its physical one, a box of blessed wood, sealed with the sigils of the Elohim.

But tonight, tonight, for some reason, the demon was near uncontrollable. Since sunrise, it was possessed of an energy they had never seen, and the priests began to tire, under constant psychic attack, seemingly from the beast itself, as well as from… somewhere beyond.

Judeai arrived at the massive crystal door to the compound, joining Anaktion, already guarding it.

"Have you seen anything?"

"Not yet," Anaktion said, as she scanned a bank of screens and monitors. "I sent Izanthar out, but she has yet to return."

"I have a bad feeling," Judeai said.

"So do I, strangely," Anaktion said.

They could do nothing but wait. And so, they stood guard, waiting, waiting, for what they felt would be inevitable.

Attack.

From Satan's emissaries on earth.

Led by one man.

The Babylonian.

"Do you see anything?" Arina's voice cracked over Anaktion's transmitter, from the command center deeper inside the base.

"No, no visual, from Judeai nor I outside, nor from the monitors up here," Anaktion said.

"Wait!"

Arina slanted her eyes as she watched the holoscreen go to static.

"All cameras are out," Veldt, sitting next to her, reported.

"All satellites, or . . ."

"No. Just cameras."

"Then it's . . . "

"Yes," Veldt said. "Ready the others."

Arina turned to go, away from the control room, then turned back to her fellow Sikari warrior.

"But how? Here?" Veldt asked. "They don't have the power to get past . . ."

"The Thule don't," Veldt said. "But someone they're with does."

Veldt was left alone, shutting the massive steel door to the command center as Arina zipped from the room, her lithe warrior's body clad, like the rest of the thirty-three Sikari within the underground complex, in their traditional soldier's garb, skin-tight black fitted suit complete with body armor covered in silver sigils, adorned on the left shoulder with the three red slashes of their order.

The alarm was sounded.

The warriors immediately armed themselves and girded for battle.

All at once, it came, a violent array of blasts sent downward upon the ground and pummeling into their compound, sending the ceilings dropping in upon them and sealing them in.

Then an explosion ripped apart the main entrance.

Blaster fire erupted through it, blocked by the Sikari's lightning-fast reflexes, and sent back upon the attackers, slaying the first wave of black figures swarming through. They were followed by another wave, the familiar dark metallic uniforms, emblazoned with Swastikas.

The Reichtarg.

Created by the Thule, the occult society of Nazis, in their top-secret bases in Antarctica and South America. Clones of their dead leader, Adolf Hitler, imbued with the DNA of fallen Nephilim, taken from the gigantic skeletons uncovered by their archaeologists, and empowered with dark magicks to augment their power. They were a savage, ruthless army, relentless.

And under the command of two men.

One, Shernihaza, the leader of the Nephilim, a multidimensional alien being several millennia old, who once helped rule the earth with cruel savagery, keeping humanity captive and submissive.

Captive and submissive to the most ancient of the multidimensional aliens, one of the original Annunaki to rule the earthen plane.

The master of the Nephilim. The leader of the Archons. The king of the Demiurge.

The Babylonian.

The hordes of over three hundred Reichtarg flooded into the complex, their dark swords clashing against the holy blades of the Sikari.

The Sikari were the far superior warriors. But they were dramatically outnumbered. And soon, they began to become more so, as the sheer weight of demonic force, buttressed by the sinister magicks of the Babylonian powering them, began to overcome the valiant Sikari.

The Sikari had joined in a defensive position, circled around the artifact, and they stood their ground, their swords lightning fast, slicing into the onslaught of Nazi clones, sending them collapsing to the floor in a hail of blood and flesh piling up around them. Dozens kept coming, a black horde, and as they did, slowly, the Sikari began to succumb to the sheer numbers. New blaster fire from the Reichtarg and an oppressive negative energy spell created by The Babylonian and Shernihaza began to stun and slow the Sikari warriors, enough for the Reichtarg blades to find their flesh, and, ultimately, strike them down.

Before long, the Sikari were greatly outnumbered, still battling courageously, but facing off against what seemed to be an endless sea of darkly garbed clones, a torrent of blaster fire and razor-sharp blades stabbing at them from all angles.

After a valiant battle, Judeai and Anaktion were the only two left.

"Destroy them!" The Babylonian howled. "Destroy the infidels who dare to defy me!"

Shernihaza stepped forward, holding out a hand to halt the Reichtarg.

The Reichtarg backed up, and, with a sardonic grin, Shernihaza willed his grotesque helmet about his head, a vile and sinister countenance of ebon and crimson that echoed the head of a jackal, with gold bands about the ears. In his hands were two circular swords ripe with blades spiking from them. He leapt into battle with unfettered joy and cruelty, savagely slicing into Sikari. They battled with strength and nobility, but both were drained from the long fight, and Shernihaza was more powerful than both. Dueling them to the death, he overpowered them with his Nephilim magicks and swordplay.

But just as she was about to die, Anaktion flung her consciousness into the computer grid of the compound. From the command center, Veldt received the warning and knew she was the only warrior remaining. A distress signal was sent out, along with all data from their computers. In less than three minutes after all the data was sent away without a trace, the command center would be destroyed by a magnetic field which would engulf the room upon completion of the sequence.

Once all the data was gone, as the self-destruct sequence began, Veldt placed her helmet upon her head, filled both hands with Sikari steel, and marched out, to face the blade of Shernihaza, and meet her fate.

She would triumph tonight, over the most powerful of the Nephilim, and the lord of the Demiurge, or she would die in glory attempting to stop them from taking the Oculus Box.

Stopping them from reclaiming the stone of power for the Demiurge.

Stopping them from allowing The Babylonian to harness his full power once more, his demonic familiar, to rule this world, as he once had, millennia before.

And so, Veldt walked out, her head held high.

Walked to her destiny.

And, ultimately, the destiny of their planet.

A destiny which had begun to grow increasingly darker.

# TWELVE

## New York City

## 2042

His eyes still boiling with rage, The Arimathean watched as Dorin Xerxes' dead body was bathed in flame before him, incinerating upon itself, without singeing the floor beneath it.

"He was not the first to betray me, to betray us," the Arimathean said to Vanth, "but he will be the last."

Vanth merely nodded slightly. His rage echoing that of his father.

The Arimathean turned to Vanth.

"We have all we need," he said to his son. "You know what to do."

"Yes, sir."

The Arimathean waived his hand over Xerxes' body and as he did, the flame subsided and it began to disintegrate to ash, crumbling away and drifting off, on a cold breeze that emerged from the dark shadows just beyond them.

"He made the same mistake others had," the Arimathean said. "Secrets can never be kept forever."

The Arimathean walked to the window of his penthouse, looking out over the city.

"Betrayal will be avenged, as it always has," he said, "with blood, fire, and a plague of destruction."

# THIRTEEN

## Rural France

## November 29, 1314

The hunting expedition had been surprisingly Spartan in bounty, leaving Philip and the dozen hunters about him sour and cold.

They were deep in the forest and the night had begun to follow them.

About to turn back.

When they began to hear the sounds.

They halted.

Again, a rustling, more distinct, nearer this time.

Bows were drawn and at the ready.

Silence.

Another sound.

King Phillip nodded towards a thick, wooded area that looked nearly impenetrable. The men trained their sights upon it. Waiting for the creature to emerge. Waiting for the kill, savoring those final few moments before bloodshed.

Little knowing it was only their blood which would stain the ground on this day.

The first arrows, black and burned, enchanted with dark magicks, shot out like venomous fangs from behind them, impaling a half dozen of the men, instantly piercing their hearts and killing them, their bodies collapsing, wide eyed and gurgling, to the chaos of dead, fallen leaves upon the earth.

The other six of the king's men turned and were able to get shots off from their bows, but they were empty in their deadly quest.

All of them were sliced aside by the blade of the one man who had emerged from the forest behind them.

They scrambled to pull new shots from their quivers but they were dead from the emerged executioner's own arrows, impaled like their brethren, before they could even touch a quill.

And all that remained was the king, surrounded by a carpet of fresh dead.

All that remained was the king, and the warrior before him.

The king's eyes filled with fear as he caught sight of the man, for his face was one he knew well. Stony and ragged through centuries of death and destruction, long dark hair framing eyes, smoldering and pained, deep sienna, the color of the horizon as it turned from day to night, and ringed with an ethereal gold.

He had lived for centuries, and had been the leader of many great armies of men, including the one the king had recently betrayed and slowly tortured and destroyed while the Arimathean was in exile, in lands far from here.

But not long ago, he had led a force of just 500 that conquered the savage hordes of Saladin, an army of close to 50,000 elite warriors.

He was called the Fire of God. The Immortal.

The Arimathean.

"Dieu sait qui a tort et a peche," the Arimathean growled at him. "Il va bientot arriver Malheur a ceux qui nous ont condamnes a mort."

The king recognized the words instantly, and his eyes welled with tears, his heart sunken in the poison of fear.

"You will be reunited with your fellow viper in death tonight," the Arimathean said. "The only question is if you will go through blade or magicks, as he did."

Phillip drew his sword.

"Your die is cast," the Arimathean said. "And you are cast to die."

Phillip raised his sword with two hands in defensive position, but he knew he was doomed, and he shook in fear as the Arimathean calmly stalked towards him, his eyes filled with hatred for one his order had once aided.

"Before you die, I want you to know your blood will drain from the crown and your line will be cursed to die by this same blade," the Arimathean said. "Your order will meet the same fate as my own."

The sounds of birds rustling into the sky whipped through the trees.

And before they had drawn black blades of escape across the horizon the Arimathean attacked, slicing off the king's hands, as they fell with his sword to the ground and he cried out in pain.

His scream was the last thing to emerge from his lips.

With a vicious, powerful blow, the Arimathean's blade ran through the king's chest, and the Arimathean held him aloft on it, as he looked into his eyes, the king's pain and fear meeting nothing but cold vengeance in the Arimathean's dark orbs.

"Dieu n'est pas content," the Arimathean spat at him, twisting the sword into him. "Nous avons des ennemis de la foi dans le Royaume."

The Arimathean spat upon his crown, upon his crest, three times, and then with one final, savage thrust, he ran him through and ripped the life from him.

The king's body slid to the ground, with the others.

The Arimathean spat upon the body and cursed it.

Then turned back, from the forest, to the cities.

To collect full vengeance for him and his fallen comrades.

# FOURTEEN

## Rural Ukraine

## 2026

"Read me another one, Daddy!" the little girl said, as her father closed the final page of the book.

The little girl's eyes danced in the candle light, her smile warming his heart. Her eyes were huge, round and violet, like her father's; her face soft and kind, like her mother's. Her hair the same jet black as both her parents. And although she was merely a toddler, just passed five, she was already tall and athletic for her age, like her father.

She was a gentle soul, who spent most of her days playing outside, tending to the animals with her father, or inside, drawing and making up stories with her mother.

The man leaned in, kissed her forehead, held her close.

"You know I love you so much," he said.

"I love you too, Daddy," she said, holding him tighter, her arms struggling to clasp around his muscular form.

She sighed. "Will the lights be back tomorrow?"

"I would think so," he said. "The storm should pass by then."

"Will the animals be alright?"

"They will. We've put them inside and made sure they were ok. Thank you for helping me with that, by the way."

"You're welcome. I want to make sure they're not afraid."

"Don't worry."

"Will you check on them for me?"

"I will," he said. "After you fall asleep."

She sighed. "Ok . . . " she said. "One more story?"

He chuckled, smiled, and put his hand to her hair, lightly caressing it, looking into her eyes.

"No more stories tonight," he said. "We'll have new stories to tell tomorrow."

"Ok," she said, holding him again tight.

"I love you, Daddy," she said.

"I love you too, Natasha."

He tucked her in, kissed her gently, then looked at her once more as she closed her eyes and snuggled into her bed, holding her stuffed bear tightly.

"I will always love you, Natasha."

"I will always love you, Daddy."

He stood up, blew out the candle, then walked softly out of the girl's room.

As he left the room, he passed by a window, and could hear the wind howling, outside, along with another sound, another . . . he couldn't quite make out . . .

"Did you read her another story again?" his wife asked, with a smirk, as she moved towards him, wrapping her arms around her husband.

"Not tonight," he smiled. "I'm . . . getting a little better . . ."

His wife chuckled. "It's not the worst thing in the world to want to spend more time with her," she said. "But she needs her rest."

"I know," the man said. "It's just . . . "

"I know," his wife said. "That's one of the things I love about you."

They kissed, and held each other tight.

"I love you, Pietr."

"I love you too, Natalia."

Outside there was a crack that sounded like thunder, and the solid thump of something hitting the ground.

"That didn't sound good," she said.

"No, it didn't," he said.

He reluctantly pulled away from her, slowly.

"I'll go check," he said.

He walked into the other room and got his boots and coat on.

"Hopefully it's nothing serious, or nothing that's going to impact the animals," he said.

"You did tell her you were going to check on them," his wife said.

"That is true," he said. "I'm keeping my promise."

"You always do."

He smiled.

"I love you," he said.

"I love you too," she said.

He pulled his collar up around him and opened the door, as the winter storm's tumult raged outside.

"I'll be waiting for you," she said, with a sly smile.

"Promise?" he said.

"Always," she said.

He smiled, then turned and pulled the door shut behind him as he walked outside. Along the paths he had just cleared, through the snow and the wind, harsh and horrible, but which had never had much of an effect on him. Since he was a boy. He never seemed to feel it, or at least it hadn't had the same effect on him as on others. It was the same with most aspects of physical pain or endurance or trial. He had never been anywhere near as affected by it as he had noticed other people had been. He hadn't really questioned it. Just felt himself fortunate. Until . . . several years past. A car accident. He had walked away unharmed. But . . . different. Over the following few weeks, something in him changed, something evolved, returned to him, and he knew. He knew his true identity. And he knew why he was here.

He had noticed his daughter was the same way. Although, in many ways, he noticed she echoed him. And, like him, he had noticed that she had strange feelings of precognition, odd visions, like the one she had told him about yesterday, the one he had also had, but which he had not told her he shared, in order to calm her and keep her happy.

He also thought of the other visions that had been flooding his mind. So familiar. As if he was downloading them from his own memories. And with them, in all of them, he held a different name. Not the one he had been born with, but one that he had held centuries ago.

One that he wished to remain there.

He had chosen this life. Chosen to remain here, to remain with his wife and daughter, and even moved them all to this even more secluded location to attempt to keep this life like a secret. He had remembered who he was. Remembered what he had been. But he had no desire to be that man again. Being that man would mean giving up the life he had. The life and the people he loved. And he had no desire for that. He was tired. Tired of fighting. Tired of the life he had lived before this one, for over a millennium. That had been enough time sacrificed, he thought. This time, he would keep for himself. For his wife and daughter.

He thought of that, now, thought of the omen he and his daughter shared, as he walked to the barn, noticed it was intact, fine, in good shape. He visited the animals, talked to them, made sure they were calm, then left, shutting the door tightly behind him.

It was then he noticed the howling.

Out in the forest.

Beyond the wind.

It had been a harsh winter. Food had been hard to come by, most likely, for the predators that lived beyond them, and it could embolden them, perhaps, to enter their farm, to attempt to break in, in search of food.

He returned to the barn. Unlocked the guns he had stored there.

Locked the barn back up again.

And strode into the forest, at the ready.

The wind ripped around him.

The howling still off in the distance.

The full moon lighting the forest, lighting the path.

The snow crunching under his boots, sticks cracking under his muscular weight.

It was then he saw the figure standing in the woods.

It was incredibly tall and imposing, even taller than his own 6'7" frame, although wiry rather than having his massive bulk. It was jet black, and wearing some sort of armor, of black and silver, and upon its head was a shimmering helmet that looked like the head of a Jackal.

"You did not make this easy," the figure said, "you managed to hide yourself quite well."

The helmet melted away to reveal the face of the figure, a shocking visage.

He was a strange, pale man, with tentacles of dried blood colored hair pulled back from his face. The claw of a tight widow's peak carved into his massive forehead, over razor cheekbones and jawbone carved in steel. He was beautiful and sinister. He had a shark-like countenance, eyes black, soulless, and devoid of any kindness, and within his wicked mouth were twin rows of sharpened teeth.

"We have searched long and far for you," the figure said, "Gaspar."

The name. The same name in his visions. And then, in an instant, it all came back to him, again. His past. His power. His true identity.

And that of the being in front of him.

"Shernihaza."

Shernihaza smiled widely, his jagged teeth wide over eyes alight with gleeful malice.

"At last, one who recalls, one who knows his true identity!" Shernihaza smiled. "This shall make this all the sweeter."

"I have no desire to recreate old wars," Gaspar said. "Find your own battles. I only wish to live this life in peace."

"That is admirable, Gaspar, admirable indeed," Shernihaza said. "But that is not an option."

Behind Shernihaza, a red flame erupted, a dimensional portal, and from it emerged a dozen Reichtarg, armed and ready for battle. And behind them, shambling forth and reeking with the stench of decay, The Babylonian.

"You shall find your peace in death soon enough," Shernihaza said. "We need your blood to spill tonight, Magi. Yours . . . and the blood of your daughter."

The Reichtarg leapt to attack the reincarnated Gaspar, and he shot his gun at them, quickly realizing it was useless, as the bullets bounced off their armor. Within seconds, one was upon him, slashing at Gaspar with the curved blades of the Thule. But the reflexes and strength of the Magi were too much for the Reichtarg. Gaspar quickly eluded the strikes and the gun in his hands became far more deadly without being discharged, as with one muscular blow, he cracked the being's helmet and its skull beneath it.

Gaspar quickly grabbed the fallen Reichtarg's weapons, just as two more of them had leapt towards him and slashed deep gashes into the Magi's back, weakening him and sending Magi blood falling to the snow. But Gaspar wasn't easily felled, and despite the wounds, and the swarm of Reichtarg upon him, he fought furiously, using the Reichtarg's weapons, ripping through them, slicing some clean in two, others' heads clear off, hurtling hard to the soft ground.

Within minutes, the Reichtarg were fallen around him, all dead, but at considerable price. Gaspar's body was slashed and bloody, his clothing ripped and red. He coughed and blood stained his lips.

"Impressive," Shernihaza said. "But it will do nothing but make this all the sweeter."

From twin sheaths, Shernihaza pulled two long ebonblades and leapt into battle with Gaspar. Their weapons clashed and exploded against one another in the howling storm, each slashing beyond the other's defenses, each other's blades tasting the sweet blood of the other and hungering for more.

With a furious spin and swing, Gaspar's blade caught the side of Shernihaza, slicing through his armor, sending the Nephilim leader flying back into a defensive stance, as Gaspar pressed the attack.

But as he did, The Babylonian's magicks bellowed dark flame from the ancient Demiurge's hands, engulfing Gaspar as he yelled out in pain, spinning backwards, back from the attack, allowing Shernihaza to recover.

Gaspar's vision cleared and he pushed aside the pain of the flame engulfing him, but it was too late. He raised his blades in defense, but they were too slow, and Shernihaza's dual fangs had impaled the Magi, driving through his massive frame.

Gaspar cried out in pain and with his last energy his own blades slashed towards Shernihaza, cutting gashes into his sides just through his armor. Shernihaza yelled out in pain.

"You . . . have won for now . . ." Gaspar said, as he struggled to retain the last of his strength, struggled to . . . "But I . . . will return . . ."

A sound rippled overhead. A white owl, in the trees. Flying from its perch.

And Gaspar fell to the ground, dead.

Shernihaza, breathing heavily, pulled his swords from the body.

"Quickly!" The Babylonian said. "The blood! The Blade of Drago!"

The Babylonian pulled the strange green blade from its sheathe and handed it to the Nephilim, who raised it high above the prone body of Gaspar and plunged it into his chest, causing the blade to glow green and begin sucking in the blood and energy of the dead Magi.

"Oh my God!"

The woman's scream caused both to look up, and at the edge of the forest stood Natalia, in shock.

"Kill her!" The Babylonian said. "But take the child alive!"

At the mention of her daughter, Natalia's shock turned to fear. She turned and ran, through the snow, through the forest and towards the house.

Shernihaza, slowed by his wounds, shambled after her, his long strides clearing the ground quickly, and getting to the home just after Natalia had closed and locked the door behind her.

"Natasha!" Natalia yelled. "Natasha!"

The young girl jolted from sleep.

Her mother rushed into her room.

"Natasha! Quickly!" she said. "Go to the secret place, as we showed you! Do not come out unless you hear my signal!"

The girl, groggy, rubbed her eyes quickly, grabbed her bear and scrambled out of her bed into the space, a secret compartment in the floor of her room, and shut it behind her.

Just before she did, in the other room, she could hear the front door smashed open.

Natalia, having retrieved a handgun, discharged it at Shernihaza, but to no avail. Even in his weakened state, he easily fended off the earthen weapon. She fired until the gun was empty, backing away from him.

"Prepare to join your husband in death," the Nephilim said, pulling his sword and lunging after her.

She dodged his blow quickly, scrambling around him and out the door, trying to draw the Nephilim after her, away from the house, away from their daughter. Shernihaza followed her out, his dark sword drawn, pushing himself forward, after her. She ran, looking behind her to make sure Shernihaza followed, through the snow, towards the forest.

Where the Babylonian was waiting for her, having gained the strength of the fallen Magi, his blood drained into the Blade of Drago.

"Coming to join him?" The Babylonian cackled, as he pulled the blade, glowing a bright green, from the bloodless body.

She gasped, then turned to run, but not twenty feet behind her was Shernihaza. Slowly stalking towards her.

"Did you find the daughter?" The Babylonian hissed.

"Not yet," Shernihaza said, "but we will."

He grasped his ebonblade, raising it as he advanced within a few feet of Natalia.

"But first, to add this one's useless blood to this ground," he said.

Natalia closed her eyes and quickly said a prayer.

Little knowing it would be answered.

The ebonsword of the Nephilim shrieked downwards, but a mere foot from the head of Natalia, it was stopped in flight, with a vicious clash of steel.

Stopped by the Trinity sword of the Arimathean.

The Arimathean's sword shoved upwards, pushing Shernihaza's blade away, and sending the Nephilim flying backwards. With a flash, the Arimathean's other hand grasped the black and silver sheath of Soulsfire and the holy sword of S'iam B'ala erupted in blue flame, the Arimathean leaping towards Shernihaza, the Nephilim barely able to throw up his second ebonblade in defense to the Arimathean's dual sword attack.

The Arimathean was relentless, punishing the Nephilim warrior and sending him back, back, until with one mighty swing, the Trinity sword shattered one of Shernihaza's ancient ebonblades, as the Nephilim was flung nearly ten feet from the Magi by the explosion of occult energy from the ages-old weapon's destruction.

The Arimathean was likewise stunned by the explosion and sent flying backwards, but landed on his feet and sprung in the direction of Shernihaza, before facing a wall of flame engulfing him, from the dark magicks of The Babylonian.

Raising Soulsfire to block the flames, he was able to call forth a frigid breeze to quell the hellfire and pull it into the holy blade's light. But the distraction had worked, as the Babylonian had hoped it would, allowing Shernihaza to recover and scramble back towards the Babylonian, who had opened a dimensional gate to hasten their escape.

"Shernihaza!" The Babylonian called out, as the gate opened in a fiery halo around him and he entered it.

The Nephilim leapt towards the gate, but the Arimathean lurched forward to barely catch the bottom of the demon's leg as he was being pulled into the time portal.

Shernihaza turned and swung his blade at the Arimathean, but the eternal warrior raised his own weapon to block the blow. However, the force of the weapons' clash caused the Arimathean's grip on Shernihaza to weaken and slip. Within the time portal, between dimensions, The Babylonian sensed the opportunity, and sent a wave of blood and fire at the Arimathean, powered by the morass of negative energy within the portal. It scalded the eternal warrior and with a mammoth push, shoved him back, and away from Shernihaza, allowing the Nephilim to escape.

The portal quickly shut, and only a fizzling flame remained, before it, too, faded to a wisp of smoke.

The Arimathean, burned and in pain from the attack, had been flung back hard against the snowy ground. He rested a second, gaining his strength, then he rose and looked to Natalia, who had collapsed, crying, thrown over the fallen body of her husband, holding him.

He walked over to her and kneeled, putting his hand on her shoulder.

"I'm sorry," he said. "I'm sorry I didn't get here earlier. We weren't sure where . . . He had hidden you, too well . . ."

The woman nodded. Still sobbing as she laid down next to her husband's body, her arms around him.

The Arimathean stood up above her, above the body, in the cold forest, where the fallen, bloodless body of his friend laid cold and quiet. He looked down on the face of his friend, still and dead, frozen in pain, and the Arimathean's heart sank.

He had only wanted a life of peace.

The life he deserved.

A prayer unanswered.

Melchior.

Now Gaspar.

And now, only one, one of the original Magi, remained.

Only one.

To return to earth. To help protect it from the evil closing around it.

One. The first. The most powerful.

Balthazar.

# FIFTEEN

## New York City

## 2042

The shrouded moon barely lit the crags of the oozing corners of the city.

It was well past midnight. The streets dead. The city's occupants locked into their tombs until morning, synthetics pulsing through their bodies to bring sleep, virtual reality worlds transforming their small, dire dwellings into somewhere else, somewhere good, that they could imagine one day being.

Anywhere but here.

Evening prayers of escape carried on the wings of technology.

The howls of the warring packs echoed through the streets, concrete capillaries littered with broken glass, garbage, blood, and the remains of the days prior.

The drones hovered overhead, silently, keeping the chipped in order.

The holograms flashed adverts, commands, instructions to what traffic remained, those that dared to be out in the morass this late.

In the bowels of the night, one man found himself without shelter, and seemingly too disoriented and incoherent to recognize his need for it.

He was tall and gaunt, thick with sweat and dirt that clung to the loose confines of his hospital gown. The sweat brought that little clothing tight and stuck to his body. His hair was long and dark, and his skin nearly as ebon and impenetrable as his mane, but through the thrash of locks his gaze, his eyes a striking amethyst and silver, pierced in strange and ethereal fashion.

He could not remember his name. He could not remember who he was. Or how he had gotten into the hospital. The sanitarium. The prison. He could not remember how he had escaped. But he had. He had stumbled out, bleeding and in pain from where he had ripped the electrodes from his flesh, from where he had torn the chip from his arm, digging it out with the sharpened edge of the metal from the electrodes, with the jagged edges of his nails.

His hands were still warm and caked with blood, his eyes still watering from . . . whatever had happened.

He . . . didn't know.

He . . . didn't know . . .

His mind had once been little but a fog, but for a while now, a while he couldn't fathom or remember for how long, it had been churning, churning.

At first in the distance he saw clouds darkening, gathering, into a storm that became increasingly violent, increasingly unstoppable.

And then . . . it happened.

And then . . . and now . . . he began to clear.

He began to clear.

His mind began to clear.

But . . .

No.

It was still so foggy.

Still so dark, cloudy, murky.

But he could tell.

There was something behind it.

Something waiting to be freed.

Something . . .

He heard the howling grow nearer and some instinct told him, some voice, to seek shelter, to try to find something, anything. Anything to protect . . .

He collected mountains of garbage and refuse, pushed it into a corner along the side of a building, to form some form of crude wall, something to protect him, something to make it look as if he could blend in, beneath it.

But even as his hands shoveled the disgusting mess about, caking his forearms and stinging his wounds, he found it was too late.

"Meat! Meat! Meat! Meat!"

He stopped.

His voice eclipsed by the cackles. The howls.

The howls, echoing through the streets.

Of the pack.

A dozen.

Maybe more.

It was hard to tell, in the darkness and scattered light.

The bare flicker of the traffic holograms and the light of the moon was barely enough to reveal the predators surrounding the man.

But for the most part, all he could make out of the figures hurtling around him, screaming, and laughing, were shadows, and the glimmer of blades and chains, the flicker of cruel eyes and sharpened teeth.

The man was frozen, frightened, his head bobbing about frantically, waiting for the first attack.

"Are you ready for us?" a female voice slithered from the darkness.

"We're ready for you," another deeper voice growled from the pack, then blazed into a demonic cackle.

A flashlight clicked on, held under the face of one of the attackers, illuminating his gaping maw and frenzied eyes. Blood dripped from his sharpened, filed teeth, his skin painted in a bizarre mask.

The light reflected off the steel of the pack's weapons.

Knives.

Switchblades.

Machetes.

Vintage implements of attack, the type favored by the gangs which terrorized this part of the city, short claws of sadism meant to prolong the pain and suffering of their victims, which brought them nothing but pleasure and laughter.

"He looks delicious," a female member of the pack purred, as another one cackled.

The leader of the pack let out a bloodthirsty scream and threw the flashlight to the ground, the glass smashing against the concrete as the blur of bodies flew at the man engulfed in the darkness.

The man felt their blades slash at him, seeking his flesh, searing his skin, ripping at it, slicing it, a little at a time, and then they would withdraw.

To make him afraid, first.

To make him beg.

To make him cry.

Succumb.

Plead.

Before, finally, they would decide whether to torture or destroy him.

This he knew, suddenly, in his head, as he could hear their thoughts, felt them slimy and disgusting oozing towards him. But how? How could he? How could he read their minds? How could he hear the same when he was in the sanitarium, hear the thoughts of the doctors, the orderlies, again coming to medicate and abuse him, disregard him, until he could take no more? Until, driven by that storm, he felt a welling inside, felt an energy that seemed both alien and incredibly familiar.

"Fresh meat!" A diabolic laugh growled forth as one of the blades made solid contact with the man's torso and left a slice of flesh on the predator's blade, making the man cry out in pain, but not in fear.

In anger.

The predators circled tighter around their prey, thinking him ripe, but within the man a lightning bolt had ripped apart the firmament of his mind and his body suddenly boiled with fire, with heat, and his eyes began to glow brilliant silver.

"What . . ." one of the predators hissed, shocked, and then he lunged forward to attack, to kill.

Only to be killed.

With superhuman speed and strength, the man in the gown grabbed the predator's arm, twisted it, and thrust the attacker's own weapon soundly into his chest, causing his fanged mouth to erupt in pain and blood.

Another predator lunged and met the same fate, impaled upon his own weapon as the tall, lithe figure violently retaliated.

Three others began to swarm upon the man, but they found themselves engulfed by an incandescent flame that surrounded the man like a force field and spread out to turn his nearest attackers to blackened skin and bones that dripped to the ground, and that seared the flesh of four others in his radius. The rest ran, scrambling away like roaches at the turning on of a lamp.

The flame remained a crimson shield around the man as the predators fled in pain and fear, and within the man's mind, sparks began to form and his mind began . . . to clear . . .

And with that clarity came recognition, and with it, he looked up to the drone that had so quickly taken an interest in this strange phenomenon that had erupted, and he sent a bolt of white light towards it, incinerating it.

And then the flame dissipated, as quickly as it had jolted forth, back into the man.

He looked around, panting, frantic, as he could hear the sirens, could feel the pulse of them through the electronic grid around him, a matrix he could sense with greater clarity with every passing moment.

He grabbed clothing off one of the few corpses not fully incinerated and put it on. Then, using his newly rediscovered power he consciously masked himself from the drones converging upon his location by scrambling their signals.

Then, he fled, running through the streets, into the night, deeper into the heart of the forbidden, diseased area of the city.

He ran without fear.

Without abandon.

And suddenly, for the first time in the thirty-three years of his existence, he ran, he existed, without doubt.

Because, now, he knew.

He knew.

And in waves, it began, began to return to him.

Shards.

Pieces.

And a larger canvas, just out of his sight.

But, he could tell, if he could just keep moving, keep trying to bring it into focus, then it would return to him. And he would know. He would finally know. Finally know who he was.

And so, he ran, looking for shelter, looking for a place where he could rest.

A place where he could begin to bring that picture into focus.

# SIXTEEN

## Aegean Sea, near the Island of Patmos

## 95 AD

They were all dead.

With the execution of James the Just, the last of the eleven, all, were gone.

Some by natural causes.

Others . . . not.

Most . . . not.

Magdalene remained in exile.

But he could not.

He could not remain apart from the fray.

He had to return.

To save the only one remaining.

His friend.

Her mentor.

John.

The one men called the Revelator.

The Revelator had been kept alive, when so many others had been slain, so that the Romans could torture him, could attempt to peel away his secrets like delicate flesh.

But much as his physical body showed a supernatural resilience, so did his mind and heart, so did his spirit, and the secrets remained, locked within him.

For a short while, six decades prior, there had been peace.

The Christ had risen. The Romans remained in power, but remained cautious, fearful, on the heels of their defeat at the hands of the Magi. The hellgates had closed, however briefly, kept locked as the Christ still walked the earth. And so, the power of Satanus had diminished considerably, the diabolic voices so strong in the heads of those who walked the path of evil had grown softer, and even disappeared with some.

It was a halcyon time.

And then, it changed.

The Christ's human body could no longer contain the power it held, it could no longer exist on this mortal plane, and so, on a beam of light, it was taken, to a massive orb in the clouds, and he was gone.

Leaving those around him behind.

For a while, the halo effect remained.

And then, it changed.

The darkness began, once more, to creep in.

The voices diminished grew louder.

The Romans, and those others in power among them, grew bolder, seeing how the tides had begun to shift.

And before long, there was rebellion.

There was war.

There was torture.

There were incarcerations and killings.

The Arimathean and Magdalene had long since left the lands of their birth, having gone shortly after the ascension of the Christ, to the land of Gaul, in a small, secluded, mysterious area they called Merovingia.

Word filtered to them of the conflicts, the rebellion, and the eventual destruction of the uprisings.

For many years, they had remained apart from it.

But no longer.

The Revelator had managed to avoid capture and remain occluded for the clear majority of the conflicts. He knew of their nature and their futility and recognized that his path was apart from them, and so he remained away, hidden with the sacred and powerful materials he, the Arimathean and Magdalene, had hidden away, even apart from the secret society of warriors in which they were trained, the Silent Hand.

It was only through subterfuge, cunning and supernatural means that the Romans could locate John the Revelator. And it was only through that same power, predominantly wielded by a trio of warlocks dubbed the Darokkhai, were they able to capture him and keep him in captivity while they tortured him, hoping to peel the entrails of his mind away, pull apart the bars and get to the location of the occult materials, and steal the knowledge he alone held.

When the Arimathean heard of his capture there was no hesitation.

Magdalene had grown older, weaker. She, for all her power and strength, for all the magic she had mastered, was still human. And while her aging process had slowed, far, far more slowly than the average human, she remained best left behind, under protection of their children who had been trained as warriors by her and their father, one who was only part human, part Magi.

The Arimathean.

He, like the Revelator, was far from mortal.

And so, he knew, his friend would not soon die, regardless of the torture inflicted upon him.

Torture would not work on one who could walk between worlds. Who could will his spirit out of his body.

He knew he would still be alive.

Alive for him to save.

The Arimathean used no subterfuge, had no respect for his opponent. He ripped through the Roman prison leaving a trail of corpses behind him. He had grown exponentially stronger in his power as a Magi in a remarkably short time and even the Darokkhai were little challenge for him. He scythed through his opposition, a force of nature, making his way to the Revelator, whose mind had fractured, tenuously grasping its last remaining scraps of lucidity and sanity. His mind had left his body repeatedly to survive the torture and with the extended time spent in the nether worlds was finding it difficult to moor back in the earth's dimensional reality.

The Arimathean broke him out and they made their way out of the city, through darkness, to the edge of land lapped by sea.

The Arimathean performed a ritual upon him, putting a necklace of sacred gems around his neck to help him heal. Then he placed him in a boat, on an area heavy with fabrics and cushions to give him comfort. He then placed a silken sheet soaked in medicinals around him, and they set off, on the Aegean sea.

"Rest, my friend, you are safe," the Arimathean said, as he watched over the once-powerful man, so frail and wounded, burned and bleeding from head to toe.

The Revelator nodded, drinking deeply from the water he had been offered. But he could barely rest. He would nod off for a few seconds before jolting awake with explosive force and wild-eyed words which were cryptic even to the Arimathean's ears steeped in clandestine languages.

"A demon's eye, silver and all-seeing . . . it arrives on a ship of stars a million skies apart . . . "

"A pale horse rises . . . rises in a withered scroll from the sand . . . and in his hand three keys and three daggers . . ."

It cut the Arimathean deeply to see his friend in such pain, to see him writhing and damaged, this person who had done so much good for this world, for these people.

The Revelator would periodically grasp at his arm and demand his gaze, demand he hear his words.

"You are alone, but not alone, there will be others you discover, some to be trusted and others who will betray . . . " the

Revelator pushed forward. "But you cannot leave this fight . . . you cannot, or you will only lose . . ."

The Arimathean closed his eyes, calling forth a halo of energy upon their craft. It would soothe and heal his friend, but more importantly ease and partially cleanse his memory, of the pain he suffered, of the prison his mind found itself in. He may not remember how he had gotten to the island. But once there, he would be better able to heal.

The Revelator slept.

Leaving the Arimathean alone, upon the water, alone with his thoughts, as he guided them to refuge, to exile.

On a secluded island.

An island called Patmos.

# SEVENTEEN

## Paris, France

## 1599

Into the midst of the candlelit enclave, a battle room wide and fortressed in marble, the sliver of a man dropped, clad in a white so brilliant it seemed to glow against the indefinite light. He held in his hand a wooden scabbard, carved with various sigils of silver and gold, and with a quick move it leapt to his hand and erupted into a blade of sacred flame, indigo and pale blue.

The black-swathed reptilian figures about the room were shocked, disquieted for just a half-second at his arrival, but quickly recovered and began circling him, closing in on their quarry.

They were bony and serpentine, clad in ebon battle garb that allowed for the wisp of movement while snaking tight at the curve of muscles twitching in anticipation of battle. Their swords were drawn and ready, ebonblades, with worn ruby quartz handles grasped tight, emitting violet black columns of flame in a distinct fang, unholy swords with the power to disrupt and dismiss supernatural flesh and inflict blinding pain and death to humans in direct proportion to their level of fear.

The white-clad man amid them stood stoic.

He scanned the room, watched as they advanced upon him.

Until, at the last moment, as they were mere feet away, he assumed a defensive stance, girding himself for battle.

The first rushed him, and he quickly and deftly avoided the attack with an economy of motion that allowed him to just as easily slip from the attacks of two others, whose flailing blades jolted two other advancing attackers into death with a swing of his blade.

The ivory figure leapt high into the air, spinning and hovering, as four more sent their swords whirring in the direction of the space he had been in, only to find their companions, sending more to the ground, limp and unmoving.

Scampering across the wall, defying gravity, the glowing wraith hit the floor with the grace of a leopard before slicing through the ranks of the serpentine demon throng, their swords just missing him, finding only each other, until only two ebon-clad fighters remained, cautiously advancing on the white figure standing calmly between them, measuring their paths of attack.

Avoiding the pitfalls of their companions, the two attacked not in unison, but as individuals, the first rapidly slicing an irregular pattern in the air before his target, attempting to distract and disorient him, before making a swift jab inward at his heart.

But in one lightning fast movement, the ivory shadow slipped aside from the blade, forcing the attacker off balance, allowing the man in white to grasp his wrist, and in one deft, expert twist, enabled him to wrest the ebonblade from the reptilian's grasp.

Now armed with two blades, the ghost spun in a furious arc, striking down both of his remaining predators, and standing alone, amidst the fallen.

With a thought, he dispatched the ebonblade into its ruby quartz sheath, and flung it across the room.

At that moment, a crow cried and a gong sounded, and a stone portal opened at the far end of the room.

Emerging from behind the ancient gateway was another warrior, larger than the rest, yet still with the same thin, wiry gait.

He was swathed in warriors' robes of the same cut, but colored a deep crimson, with the same cowl hiding his face, only the crimson glimmer of his reptilian eyes visible in a sliver of shadow.

In his hand was a handle of onyx and silver runes, far more ancient than any ebonblade, a sword of legend, of demonic power, a sentient weapon only able to be wielded by a warrior of the most diabolical order. In an instant, it was ablaze, a majestic plume, a massive deadly claw of crimson flame.

The warrior in red leapt towards the man in white, sword raised to strike. At the last moment, the ivory figure darted through the air, out of his grasp, as the red warrior dropped to the ground, his blood-colored blade swung in a mighty swath.

The white figure leapt to a bejeweled chest at the fore of the room, and with a swipe of sacred flame from his hand, it opened, revealing an ancient crystal that glowed an eerie neon green, securing the chain between their two dimensions and acting as a portal between them.

In an instant, the red warrior attacked and the two swords met in a brilliant burst of light that crackled and burst like thunder.

With an echo of strikes and parries that left fading halos of light about the two warriors, the blades slashed and crashed into one another with increasing fury, the pair of fighters captured in a dance of deliberate destruction, each attempting to get the better of the other in an increasing frenzy.

Until with one Herculean swing, the red warrior's blade dislodged his opponent's blade from his grasp, sending it sailing across the temple floor.

Seizing upon his opening against his unarmed opponent, the crimson-clad demon swung downward without a second's thought.

And within that moment, his prey eluded him, slicing away from the fiery blade as the white warrior scissored a leg across the shins of the red warrior pitched forward, sending him stumbling to the ground.

Quickly gaining command from his opponent's fall, the white warrior outstretched a long-fingered hand and with a magnetic force the warrior's lost wooden scabbard was once more in his hand and it erupted with blue holy flame. The crimson warrior's sword rang down but it was blocked and parried as the white warrior leapt to his feet. The crimson demon struck again, but was once more thwarted. With a muscular blow, the reptilian was knocked to the floor.

The white warrior stood above the red warrior and with an invisible, magnetic pull of unstoppable force, the blade handle was yanked from the hand of the stunned, fallen demon and spun fast and sure into the grasp of the white warrior, where its flamed blade was extinguished, the handle flung to the far end of the temple.

The red warrior, dazed and fallen, sat up slightly, reached up, and removed his cowl, revealing a sharp, dark face, reptilian, half-human, half-lizard. He tried to attack the white warrior, tried to claw at him with his razor-sharp talons, but the warrior was too quick, and with a mighty swing of his indigo holy sword, he sliced back the demon's attack. With another herculean blow into the demon's chest, the demon exploded in an acrid black smoke as it was sent skittering back to the nether realms with his reptilian brethren.

The throne room cleared of the demonic entities, the white warrior focused his attention upon the emerald crystal, which began to growl and moan as reptilian ebony figures whirled about inside it, trying to enter the earthen dimension.

But with a hurricane strike downward, the ivory warrior's holy blade shattered it, destroying it, and the link between the dimensions, sending the ashen souls of the reptilians back to their nether world.

The warrior in white removed his cowl.

To reveal a harsh, carved countenance, and eyes dark sienna pierced with a crown of golden thorns around them.

The face of the eternal warrior.

The Arimathean.

Looking down at the destruction, he raised a hand and the shards of the dimensional crystal lifted from the ground, hovering, then swirling together, slowly, then increasing in velocity. The Arimathean held open a dark velvet pouch, and the pieces swirled into it. When they had all been cleared, he affixed the pouch back onto his belt.

And as he did, he was stunned to hear, behind him, the sound . . . of two hands clapping.

The figure stood at the end of the room, a smug smirk upon his face.

He was tall and thin, strikingly handsome, with high cheekbones and delicate, elfin features. Huge, almond-shaped eyes of a clear blue, cream-colored skin, and short, light blonde hair, that haloed his face like a crown of fire.

"What are you doing here?" The Arimathean asked.

"I knew you would be here," the thin man responded. "You don't think I have my own eyes and ears within the Silent Hand?"

"What do you want, Lucifer?"

The thin man sighed. "You know I hate that name."

The Arimathean shrugged.

"I've been waiting for a moment to speak with you," the thin man said. "I've been watching you a while, as you know. I think there's something you need to see."

The thin man held out his hand to reveal a dark indigo stone, flecked with silver stars, which glimmered bright, opening a widening light blue gate before him.

"Come with me," he said.

The Arimathean hesitated.

The thin man glided his arm in display of the carnage of the room. "Unless you'd prefer this company," he said, "although I think you've been to this party far too many times."

The Arimathean, wary but curious, followed the thin man through the dimensional portal opened by the Centauri stone.

They emerged from the wormhole into an ancient castle, torches upon the wall and intricate tapestries hung spiraling to the high ceilings, carved with intricate tableaux of ancient Mesopotamian hieroglyphs and painted with vibrant colors.

"Why did you bring me here?" the Arimathean asked.

But the figure merely turned and walked, past a red curtain, as he pushed a stone upon the wall to open a secret entranceway to a hidden room.

Leaving the door open behind him for the Arimathean to follow him, he casually sauntered in.

The Arimathean walked into the room, and as he did, a massive steel and stone wall fell behind him, shutting him in, as the room fell into total darkness.

The Arimathean immediately drew his blades, expecting attack.

The Arimathean's eyes adjusted and he could make out vague shapes, including the one of the man he had followed, far against the wall. But no other signs of enemies. No soldiers. No demons. No one to battle.

The figure raised both of his hands and instantly the room was filled with light, as an array of massive crystal globes embedded in the columns of the walls became illuminated.

Displaying a strange sight.

A monumental . . . library.

Bookshelves lined the walls, filled with tomes that were ornate and ancient.

A stairway, on the left-hand side at one end of the room, led downward, to where, he did not know. The hall they were in opened to a huge room beyond it, likewise packed with various books and scrolls. And at various points on the walls, near the crystal globes, were small rose-colored crosses.

On the far end of the space, in the larger room beyond this one, was a mosaic inlaid on the wall, of broken glass and pottery, all various shades of red and rose, in the shape of a cross.

"Welcome," the figure said, with a smile.

The Arimathean remained stunned, suspicious, looking around.

"Don't worry, there will be no warriors emerging, no demons summoned from beyond," the figure said. "The only warrior you will be battling here is you. The only demons those you have been programmed to carry with you for centuries."

The Arimathean looked around, scanning the room, the shelves, the seemingly endless array of knowledge before him. He sheathed his weapons.

"How can I trust you?" The Arimathean said. "You are the prince of lies. Lucifer."

The figure sighed, rolled his eyes.

"Please don't call me that, that is not my name, merely an appellation attached to me by the ignorant," the figure said. "I am Enki, as you know. And you, are Josephus."

The Arimathean's eyes slanted with suspicion and surprise at the mention of his name.

"Lucifer, the light bringer, the eastern star, the illuminatus, they are all mere descriptions, of one who attempted, and still, although not as often, for he has seen the vanity of his ways, but who still attempts, in some cases, to bring illumination, to shine light, on information, on wisdom, in this world," Enki said.

"Why would I trust you?"

"I don't ask you to trust my words, but to investigate the facts, the information provided, and make up your own mind," Enki said. "That is all I have ever asked of you and your people."

Enki strode to a weathered tome upon the wall, pulled it out, blew the dust off the top of it. The word "Zoroaster" shone brilliantly in gold upon it. He set it down, conspicuously, for the Arimathean to take up, and discover. Next to another, even more weathered volume of gold and leather, bearing the name "Mithra."

He cracked open the dark brown, weathered leather of its cover. "We are not so different, you and I," Enki said. "But that you shall discover."

Enki set the book down. He reached into a black, velvet pouch on his belt, and within his palm he held a stone of indigo that danced with silver stars.

"I'll leave you now," Enki said. "You'll find everything you need to survive in this underground world. But, more importantly, if you choose to discover it, you'll also find everything you need to live."

The Arimathean scowled.

"You're going to leave me in this prison?"

Enki smiled.

"You have been in prison for almost two millennia," Enki said. "I am giving you the key to escape it."

Enki took another Centauri stone from a pouch on his belt and left it on one of the shelves.

"Come and go as you wish," Enki said. "Your only limits are those of your mind, your imagination and your will."

With his words lingering in the air, Enki smirked and a blossom of blue lightning burst from the Centauri stone in his hand, enveloping him in an oval of light, which ebbed and waned, shrinking to sparks, as Enki disappeared.

But even in his wake, the lights remained.

Illuminating the walls of knowledge, and the path ahead of the Arimathean.

# EIGHTEEN

## Salem Town, Massachusetts

## 1693

Usually left to the province of dark whispers and frigid ghost tales on sleepless nights, the secret vault of the Mathers was subject to much conjecture among the townspeople, but its reality was far worse. It was a miserable tomb for those unfortunates who were condemned to it by the religious elders of the town, awaiting their eventual death by flame or water, a death which often seemed welcome compared to the suffering imposed by their imprisonment.

Dank and raw, down in the depths of the earth beneath the prison, the vault housed those who were deemed the worst of sinners, those who were judged to bear the mark of the one they called Satan himself. Those they found to be witches and warlocks, men and women who were judged to be in league with the darkest of supernatural forces.

Only a few could enter the secret vault. Those that guarded it were hand-picked by the Mather himself, and only those who were deemed pure of body and spirit were allowed inside as guardian or visitor.

The priest had arrived mysteriously, from out of town, but he bore the appropriate papers and seemed to be of regal bearing. He was strikingly handsome, with ice blue eyes and golden hair, which framed an angelic face. He gave the right answers and was sufficiently obsequious and uncannily persuasive to the town elders to allow him passage into the vault. He was led by one of the few church elders who knew where the vault was and could gain entry to it, through the hidden passageways beneath the prison and past the various locked doors that led to the deepest, most heinous bowels of its vermin-infested pit.

As the two descended down strange corridors and beyond ancient wooden doors, their paths illuminated only by the torches they carried, one could not help but notice the contrast of the two.

The elder seemed tight and shrunken as a prune, pursed, gray, and sour, with squinted eyes and wiry hair beneath a tight black hat that matched his barren black suit upon his stout, plump body.

The priest, looking sharp and young, in his light, billowing robes, and finery, supernaturally handsome, with high cheekbones and striking blue eyes beneath short, light hair.

"And why, may I ask, is there such interest in this prisoner from such a higher authority?" the elder asked of the priest.

"The fact you have him locked so far beneath the earth does not answer that question?" the priest replied, with a cocked eyebrow.

The elder had questions, but, suddenly, felt cold and went silent, and for a moment he thought of stopping, and not allowing the priest to go any further. There was something about the look in the priest's eye that made his spine melt, but he could not stop. For some reason, one he could not grasp, he felt compelled, almost beyond his control, to continue.

They stopped at the last gate. It was unlocked. The door opened.

"Thank you," the priest said, with a smile.

The priest entered the room, and the door shut quickly, locked, behind him. Only a feeble torch lit the room, sputtering.

With a snap of the priest's fingers, the flame blossomed like a rose bush in spring and the room became awash in light.

The elder, seeing the sudden illumination, filled with fear, and rumbled up the stairs.

The priest chuckled to himself.

"Ridiculous," he said.

The lone figure imprisoned remained seated in the corner of the room. He only briefly looked up at the priest. The man didn't move. He was heavily muscled and rugged, but unkempt and possessed of wild hair and a violent outbreak of a beard falling over his torn clothing.

His face was stony and distant, his eyes a storm of earth and gold.

The Arimathean.

"Hello, Enki," the Arimathean said.

"Thank you," Enki replied. "You know I so despise that other title."

The Arimathean nodded, barely, in slight acknowledgement.

"You don't seem surprised to see me," Enki said.

"I'm not," the Arimathean said.

Enki looked around at the dirt and squalor of the room, the vermin scampering about it. The blood stains against the wall from where others had been beaten. Others who had been marked as witches, warlocks or worse.

"How ironic," Enki said, "they create this tomb for those they falsely accuse of being demons and in doing so become demons themselves."

He looked back at the Arimathean. "And they let me in here with a smile," Enki said. "Or, what passes for one in this dour depression hole."

The Arimathean remained silent.

"And they call themselves men of God," Enki said. "They call themselves Christian."

Enki looked down to see a child's doll, discarded, at an outer edge of the room.

"We both knew the last Christ, and I hardly think he would find this a kind approximation of his message," Enki said, picking the doll up. "He said a lot about helping the poor and suffering. A lot about love and kindness. Nothing I recall about treating them with cruelty or unjustly accusing them of witchcraft."

Enki dropped the doll to the floor near the Arimathean.

"But I think we both also know that his words and his message have been a bit, misinterpreted and edited considerably, over the years," Enki said.

The Arimathean merely looked over at the doll and scowled.

"Why do you remain?" Enki said. "We both know you could break out of here easily. And, for that matter, we both know they shouldn't have been able to capture and imprison you in the first place. Unless you let them."

"Perhaps I remain here in penance for my sins, or perhaps to just escape."

"How many times have they tried to execute you?"

"Twice."

"They cannot kill you. And once they truly discover that, they'll merely leave you here to rot even longer than you have been."

The Arimathean merely looked down.

"Why do you bother with them?" Enki said. "I was once like you, filled with faith in them, wanting to give them their freedom, their independence, and so I did, only to be betrayed. Only to have them turn on me. And worse, they turned on me and ran to the embrace of the one who put them in their prison. And even worse, they listened to him as he cast me as the villain, to prevent them from trusting me again. To create their own prisons."

Enki crouched down, thought of sitting down, but a disgusted look soured his face.

"This is repulsive," Enki said. "You deserve far, far better than this."

He crouched down on the pads of his feet, across from the Arimathean.

"I'll leave you with a few things to think about," Enki said. "You've read the old testament?"

"Yes, of course. Many times."

"Haven't you ever wondered why an all-powerful god would care so much about animal sacrifices, or the purity of the animals killed in his name? Why would he care so much about blood spilled for him? What would he need blood for?" Enki said. "And have you ever asked yourself why that god was so directly active in the lives of people during that time but after Jesus' arrival, in the new testament, he wasn't?"

The Arimathean nodded.

"There is only one God," Enki said. "Only one all-powerful God of the universe. People should be careful of those who claim otherwise. There are no gods, plural. No demons. And while there are humans who have referred to me as both, I am neither. We are all mere beings, creations of the one true God. The only difference between us and the humans are that we are further along the evolutionary chain and the dimensional spheres. Just as you appear a god to the ants which crawl below you, we are gods to these people. And so, like the ants, these humans fall, thinking themselves dependent upon our mercy for their lives to be spared. And like you, standing above the ants, your likelihood of sparing them is entirely dependent upon your predilection to cruelty or whether they bite and attack you."

Enki turned his head to hear men gathering and talking with violent tones on the other side of the door.

"Case in point," Enki said, sauntering over to the door, before looking back at the Arimathean. "Did I do anything to deserve such churlish treatment? Have you? All I've done is come to visit an old friend."

The Arimathean scoffed. Enki stood by the door and listened to the commotion outside it.

"So much fear, they have," Enki said. "And all shadowed by the greatest control mechanism of all. The fear of death."

Enki shook his head and sighed. "If you control a man's belief in death you control his belief in life."

The Arimathean listened as the mob of men coagulated outside the door, growing louder.

"Remember, Josephus, you create your own life," Enki said. "Free will is the greatest power upon this planet. These men could live in peace. They could merely decide to let us leave, let me leave. Or they could attack me and suffer the consequences. I have done nothing but walk in here and talk to you. There is no reason for them to attempt to kill me or condemn me. And yet here they are, looking to do both. Of their own free will. They could walk away, and live in peace. Or they could attack me and force me to defend myself. What will they do? What . . . will . . . they . . . do?"

The door locks began to click open as the men began to angrily call for hanging or burning the men inside the cell. The Arimathean watched as Enki's face lit up in anticipation.

"So predictable," Enki smirked sardonically. "Once more, I leave you in a prison of your own making, Josephus. I look forward to seeing you once again, a free man. And I hope the decisions you make bring you the peace you deserve."

The door opened slowly, the men cautiously entering as others in the back called out for the demons to be killed, slain like the others.

The men walked into the room, weapons and torches in hand, as the one leading them pointed at Enki. "You, sir, are accused of witchcraft and consorting with the devil!"

"Define consorting," Enki replied.

"What?"

"Well, technically, I have spoken to Satanus, the one you mistakenly call Satan, or the devil. So, I have consorted, so to speak, in the broadest terms. But we're hardly friends and I wouldn't say I was in league with him. In fact, it's usually been the opposite," Enki said. "I've tended to disagree with him and he's tended not to like it. Nor has he much liked me, for that matter. Nor have I really liked him, to be honest. He's rather brutish and annoying."

"He admits his guilt!" one of the men in back exclaimed. "He says he speaks to the devil!"

Enki sighed. "Obviously, you really weren't listening to what I was saying . . ."

"Hang him!"

"Burn him!"

The men raised their weapons and advanced upon Enki.

Enki raised his hands. "Gentlemen, I have been more than patient with you. And you have been less than cordial with me," Enki said. "And so, I'm about to give you exactly what you have been so desiring but have yet to witness in all your hollow, biased trials and petty condemnations. So, enjoy it, in the few seconds you'll have, before you move on to the next plane. And so, I bid you, farewell."

Just as the men were about to seize him, Enki disappeared in a bright flash of light, and transformed into a shadow of dark smoke that whipped around the men like tentacles and choked their cries of fear in their throats. His laugh echoed as the ebon cloud flew from the room in a harsh, cold wind, pulling the men with him in a wave, the door slamming behind them. The locks smashed as the door slammed shut, leaving the broken, heavy wooden portal to fly fully open, and the Arimathean could see, and hear, the massacre taking place outside his cell.

He watched as, in that dark cloud, the bodies were strangled and skinned, drowned, and burned as they had done to their victims. The Arimathean watched as they were dragged through the corridor, and could hear as they were pulled upward, up the steps, screaming in pain, the cries being snapped quiet with the sounds of necks breaking.

As the cloud whipped away pulling the men with it, a vacuum pulled the door shut behind, and it once more slammed in its moorings, before creaking slightly open.

And then, silence. But just for a moment.

And then . . .

Only the door.

Slowly, slowly, opening to the Arimathean.

Remaining open.

As his room remained filled with light.

And he looked at the door to the world outside, laying before him.

And above, outside the prison, Enki, in human form again, strode away, his white, priestly cloaks billowing behind him as he turned to see the trail of dead strewn in his wake.

"In public, they will be missed," he thought, "in private, they won't be."

He looked back at the cell.

Thought of the Arimathean.

Smiled.

"He'll thank me later," Enki said, and with a sly grin, he strode away, slowly, and confidently.

# NINETEEN

## Airspace over Midwestern America

## 2042

Their hovercraft powered by the Merceron crystal, hidden from radar, Bastian and Zinesha soared high over the plains and into the barren lands beyond, headed to Sedona.

Bastian had tried to reach the Sikari base there, but to no avail.

She dreaded the reason, but hoped she was wrong. Hoped she had been wrong.

Zinesha looked out the window at the country zooming beneath them, its geography changing in her eyes seemingly as quickly as it had changed in so many ways in the past few decades.

It had begun with California voting to secede in 2019. Led by Seattle and Portland, Washington and Oregon followed the next year, and the three joined to form the Pacific Coast Alliance, the PCA, covering the whole of the west coast.

Texas, long chafing to bolt, and unhappy with the results of the 2020 election, left in 2021, going alone. Led by New York and the old money of Massachusetts and Connecticut, the whole of New England voted to leave in 2025 after reports of widespread voter fraud in the presidential elections of 2024, after the already bitter elections of the previous two cycles. They were followed by Illinois in 2026 and Utah, forming its own sovereign Mormon state, in 2029. Colorado, after shouldering a disproportionate amount of the financial burden of the remaining states, went independent in 2030, primarily for financial reasons. Montana went its own way the same year, largely due to demand from its population, which had been pushing to form a sovereign area. Likewise, due to financial and cultural forces, Minnesota, Wisconsin, and the metropolitan Davenport area of eastern Iowa seceded in 2032 to join with Illinois to form the Northern Alliance. And the same year Arizona, New Mexico and Nevada formed a triumvirate calling themselves the New Western Alliance.

The PCA quickly became one of the most technologically advanced and financially successful countries in the world. Led by Silicon Valley scientific advances, they became energy independent, utilizing wind, wave and solar energy to completely power the PCA and export power to other parts of the country. A stunning invention to convert salt water to fresh water solved the drought problems plaguing the region and within a decade, the PCA was the second-largest economy in the world, and the richest per capita. New England, while not as booming, was likewise prosperous and likewise socially progressive, also becoming a world power economically and building particularly strong alliances with Europe. The other independent states also experienced economic rejuvenation after secession, although they were more parochial in scope, trading with the others as well as the remainder of the United States.

The remaining United States weren't as fortunate. Some areas, particularly those in the middle-west, where the population was less dense and there was already a solid amount of accumulated wealth, remained roughly the same. But many of the states which had been heavily dependent upon the federal government for help, and which had seen the amount of monies provided by that federal government shrink rapidly over a little more than a decade due to the secessions, became wastelands of poverty with grotesque gaps between the few very rich and the vast multitudes of poor and struggling lower middle class. The wreckage from natural disasters took much longer to repair. In some cases, areas were never restored, left as skeletal reminders of what they once were, becoming lawless zones infested with squatters and vermin. With many governmental regulations stripped away in those remaining states, pollution and toxins in the air, drinking water and foods became common. Consequently, health issues spiked and healthcare costs skyrocketed, further exacerbating their conditions. With education funding slashed and decimated, schools closed and literacy rates plummeted. Crime rates leapt, and with them, the populations of the privatized prison system, which was essentially used as cheap labor. Monies collected from criminal activity and petty fines increased and with the recognition of that as a revenue stream, the number of laws and regulations also spread.

And so increased support for the microchips.

Long before the secessions, the plan had been in place for the chip implants in the populace. And rather than impeding the progress on widespread chipping, the splitting of the states made it all the easier, as those behind the plan could divide and easily conquer any objections, whether with coercion, fear, or financial incentives. Several regional skirmishes and civil unrest over several years only allowed those in control to push their agenda with greater expedience and ease.

The chips were ostensibly for commercial and safety purposes. And, despite the objections of a minority that slowly dwindled, they were assimilated into the vast majority of the population within two years. It began with their implantation in dozens of "sport models" and other MK Ultra-controlled celebrities, creating a must-have trend that broke through easily to the first adaptors, and by the end of the first Christmas season, which brought with it a multitude of virtual reality games and other amenities and vanities tied in with the chips, over 60 percent of the population was on the grid. With another roughly 30 percent to join within the next year. The remaining less than ten percent were consigned to outlier status. Most of those who refused the chips ended up removing themselves from society, living in the free-range zones, or were among the packs of the unchipped, who took themselves off grid in the cities to avoid the law. But often, those with criminal intent found ways to hack the chips to use to their own benefit. Little did they know that even if they surface hacked them, there were several subsurface applications of which they weren't aware, which remained in effect and enabled them to be monitored and controlled.

As for those who opted out of the chipping system, they were allowed to freely do so. There was no need to force them, as most of the country was under massive surveillance already. In addition, several studies had determined, and the years bore these out, that those who dropped out of society just wanted to be left alone and were of no real threat.

The chips contained the data of each person, allowing them to conduct business the same way they would with a credit card, and acted as identification. But it was slowly revealed that they also acted as a means of population control and distraction. The chips emitted a frequency and chemical which prevented contraception. And they also allowed a far easier transition for humans into the web and the virtual world.

Both were eagerly embraced, as both facilitated the primary means of escape for the population – through physical pleasure or through virtual reality and gaming, slipping into custom avatars to wander virtual worlds far more pleasant for most than the ones they inhabited.

Once the chips were in and active, conception was allowed only through license. Both parents had to apply through the state, going through a battery of biological and psychological tests, counseling, and written and verbal tests, to determine if they were ready and able to handle the responsibility of parenthood. If they were determined unable to do so, yet still scored high enough, they could continue to re-apply. If they were determined to be under a certain threshold, they were put under a five-year ban. Violent criminals, hardcore addicts and the mentally and severely physically handicapped were banned from reproduction. Again, much like the implementation of the chips, this was met with a support and enthusiasm that went beyond expectations.

The three ancient secret societies of the Vendari, Sikari and Silent Hand had operations in every area of the states, as well as the world, but all of them had primary bases of operations. The Sikari operated largely out of the PCA, the Silent Hand in New England, and the Vendari in Colorado and Utah.

The fourth society, the Thule, neo-Nazi occultists, were a limited presence in the States, kept out by the trinity, and they largely operated outside the law. Utah, from the start, remained staunchly Mormon, controlled by the church, and was a western neutral zone. The Northern Alliance was the same, a neutral area in the middle of the country that lived under largely socialist principles and had, over the past few years, slowly become more under the control of a shadowy group of technologists and computer experts calling themselves the TechNoir, under the control of a clandestine computer genius who went by the name Anansi, who also had a significant presence in the Western Alliance, again, under the radar.

And at the center of them all, at the nexus of every technological and social construct, was one man, who stood outside each but was respected by all.

He had founded two of their orders, the Sikari and Vendari, and was at one point the sole reason for the continued existence of the third, the Silent Hand.

He was known as The One Who Could Not Die, The Fire of God, The Black Knight.

He had been born over 2,000 years before, a man, once, named Josephus.

Before becoming a Magi, then leaving the order.

And over two millennia he became known by another name.

The Arimathean.

Few knew the true nature and name of those he counted as his closest confidantes. But all knew the names of his closest warriors. His son, Vanth, who ostensibly led the Silent Hand, and his daughter, Bastian, who led the Sikari.

"Why are we going to Sedona?" Zinesha said.

"The place we were at, which we found destroyed, was, not long ago, the hiding spot for an oculus stone," Bastian said. "A stone which was sent first into the Northern territory and then on to Sedona, under guard of the Sikari."

"What is it?"

"An oculus stone?"

"Yeah."

"It's an ancient object of great magickal force, which contains the power of the ancient beings which once ruled this planet."

"The dinosaurs?"

"No, not quite that far back," Bastian smiled. "A group called the Demiurge."

"Sounds like a metal band."

"Might have been. I don't monitor their hobbies."

"So, who are they?"

"They were beings from another planet, another dimension, who were farther along the evolutionary chain than humans were," Bastian said. "You're familiar with the big bang theory?"

"Yeah," Zinesha said. "Huge explosion of matter that scattered universe parts everywhere and keeps going ad infinitum."

"The earth and its galaxy are somewhere in the middle of the universe. So, wouldn't it stand to figure that those on the far end, who have had a longer time in existence, would also have had a longer time to evolve?"

"Yeah."

"And so, they did, although through curiosity and need they found themselves looking for other planets, other worlds, and so they found earth," Bastian said. "To the early humans, they, with their advanced technology and power, were worshipped as gods, the same way we would be if we went back in time."

"Like the gods of ancient Egyptians or Mesopotamians," Zinesha said. "Or the Annunaki."

"Exactly like them," Bastian said. "In fact, exactly them."

Bastian looked over at the girl next to her. "You don't seem phased by this at all."

"I was raised in the free-range zones by a bunch of hippies," Zinesha said. "I was having my aura read and my chakra aligned before I could ride a bike."

"Touché."

"But, you can stop them, right?" Zinesha said. "That's why the Magi are still here, and the Sikari are still here, right?"

Bastian looked away from her, over the horizon, as they neared their destination.

"That's our hope," Bastian said.

"How many Demiurge are there?"

"There were nine primary left."

"How many are there now?"

"We're not sure. Maybe as many as six. Maybe as few as two or three."

"Why don't you know?"

"They were imprisoned in sarcophagi and hidden. Some of the sarcophagi have been destroyed. But we're not sure exactly how many."

"But who destroyed them, if not you guys?"

"Capulet."

# TWENTY

## London, England

## 1986

Frank Case walked through the silent, monochromatic underground complex, to a cold steel wall broken by a small dark screen, offering a black mirror to his calm visage as he touched his palm to the glass and it scanned his flesh with a neon green glow.

A crimson, circular glass emerged from behind a steel plate, at eye level. He looked into the viewfinder and it scanned his retina, flashing "access granted."

He punched in his six-digit code on a third screen which presented itself.

And the door to his office opened.

Where he found a familiar figure, leaned back in his chair, feet up on his desk, whistling a familiar tune.

"God, I'm sick of that song already," Case said, as he picked up a computer tablet and looked down at his messages. "Was that your doing?"

The figure smiled, raised his hands slightly and shrugged his shoulders.

"He was looking for a muse, I provided it," the figure said. "Although if you ask him, and a lot of reporters have been, it's nothing but a catchy tune and the lyrics nothing but nonsense that popped into his head."

"But of course, it isn't," Case said, motioning for the figure to get out of his chair. "And they aren't."

The figure complied, with false courtesy.

Getting out of the chair, he stood up to his full height, well over six feet tall, muscular, and thin, dressed in an immaculately tailored suit, with short, fashionably styled blonde hair. His skin was tanned and bright, his eyes bright blue, jewels in a face that seemed sculpted from marble by a renaissance artist.

"They never are," the figure replied. "The artists never realize they're merely conduits for a message that so few will recognize they understand, but that deep inside, they remember."

"Except for the avatars," Case said.

"Yes, except for them," the figure said. "But they don't last long, do they, Mr. Case?"

Case didn't look up, his face remaining down on his desk, looking over a skein of information rifling by on a computer screen built in to the large sheet of marble.

"You know that we're not the ones responsible for that," Case said. "We like artists here."

"Yes, I know you do," the figure said. "They are useful brushes for you to paint the canvas. I understand. And the avatars do prove useful, as guides, do they not?"

Case said nothing, looking up at Enki.

"We're not responsible for that either."

"Almost eight now, or is it nine? Since just after World War I. That's almost one avatar per decade," Enki said. "Someone seems to be sending a message, although someone else seems even more determined not to let it be delivered."

"Again, we have nothing to do with that."

"Neither do I, but, like you, I remain curious about it," Enki said. "We are not so different, you and I."

"What do you want, Enki?" Case said.

"Well, Frank, as I said, we're not so different, you and I," Enki said. "In a few very significant ways. And while you may not take an interest in some things, I do know you take a very keen interest in others."

Case crossed his arms and sat back in his chair, leaning back, and looking squarely at Enki, his eyes slanting and curious.

"Where?"

"Siberia. One. Most likely Shernihaza."

"We knew about that. The Russians got to it before we could. We intercepted their communications and deciphered their code. They're about to make the same mistake Reagan did. And for the same reason. Nothing we can do now. They'll find out soon enough."

"A second. Iraq. Southwest."

Case nodded. "Not surprising."

"No."

"Is that it?"

Enki smiled, picked up an ornamental crystal orb from Case's desk, looked it over.

"No," he said. "There is a third. It was found in the Amazon rainforest, under the ruins of a Mayan temple, ironically enough, which had been overgrown with a dense carpet of foliage. Funny how the earth always has its way. The Vendari discovered it. Then it passed to the Silent Hand. Then the Sikari. Then I lost track of who had it next as it journeyed through the

Americas, but now, from what I can gather, it's making its way through Europe and is scheduled to arrive in a city we both know quite well."

Case thought a moment, then his face tensed.

"Berlin."

Enki put the orb back.

"Then you know who has it now," Enki said.

"Where is it?" Case said.

"Last I was aware, Oslo," Enki said. "But you know they're trying their best to keep it from me. And you."

Case nodded.

"There are . . . plans in motion for Berlin," Case said.

"You don't say?" Enki smirked.

"You and I both know what's going to be happening in the next few years," Case said.

"And you and I both know what they want to happen," Enki said.

Case looked hard at Enki.

"Thank you for the information," Case said.

"As always, a pleasure," Enki said.

Case touched a few keys on a touch screen on his desk.

"Don't bother, I'll let myself out," Enki said, and in a flash, he transformed to a black tentacled mist which disappeared into the ventilation shaft.

Case's features were somber.

He looked down on his desk.

And then, a light emerged, illuminating his face, and the merest hint of a smile crossed his lips.

# TWENTY-ONE

## Tunguska, Russia

## 1908

It is a circuitous, storied path, a blessed journey, through the fabric of the universe. A path of almost unquestionable defiance of the odds, a charmed history, to navigate through the infinite, avoiding the elements of chaos and destruction that assail it from every direction, as it travels, as it has for centuries, along its path, towards its destiny.

It was created in this, this beautiful matrix, this eloquent pattern, this awesome symphony of cacophony from the eye of God, brought to life millennia past and set on its path by a sentience that knows no time, that only knows and encompasses, the infinite.

There have been moments when it appeared close to destruction, moments when its glittering prize was threatened, by forces unpredictable and furious, summoned and sinister, but now, it has arrived, arrived at the brilliant blue orb for which its cargo was predestined, for which its genetic code, its alchemy of chemicals and magnetic fields will create, create that which the universe has sent it to birth, set in motion on this orb that will erupt and evolve and cleanse it, for without destruction there is no rebirth.

Without destruction, there is no rebirth.

And so, it reaches the end of its journey.

This fingerprint of God.

Interlocking with another.

On an arbitrary measurement of time the inhabitants of this planet deem a day, a year, a century, a millennium, the comet ends its journey through the universe, a journey that began with an idea in the eye of God, with intention made being.

And then it begins its descent.

Countless bodies have died at this place, engulfed in flame, disintegrated by velocity and inertia, unstoppable forces meeting immovable object, protective shield moving at amazing speed. They have been ice and rock, metal and chemical, just like this one.

But not like this one.

Nothing at all like this one.

This one cleaves through the atmosphere at precisely the right angle, obeying its pattern of transit.

And then it falls, soars downward to this plane, to this planet, to this earth.

Its time and location noted by those who Watch, by those who know, by those who have been waiting for its arrival.

And so, as the time of this year, this millennium, expires, and a new one begins, its flames cleave through the sky, seen by few, but when seen, seen by those who will marvel and awe, who will attach their hopes and dreams to it, who will see it as a sign, as a herald, as a harbinger.

It will scythe across those dark skies in the eyes of few and touch down in the eyes of none, tearing through a distant and isolated area, to rip through trees and embed itself in the earth, where it will blaze and cool, and its cargo will ignite and spread.

Spread first to the flora and fauna, who will carry it, carry it, on to its ultimate hosts.

And so, it will evolve, and the web will form, upon this planet, upon this world.

And so, it will evolve, this pattern, connected to the source, to the origin, to whence it came, which connects to the universe, which connects to all, which connects to the eye of

God, that fabric of the galaxy infinite miles away yet moments apart within the field which connects it.

Connects it in a blink.

As it did millions of years ago.

When another like this, another seed of the universe, the first, made the first journey to this planet, to begin its cycle. As so many other seedlings had made the journeys to so many others. To begin the reactions that would lead to a sprawling tapestry, a canvas, of God's own creation and mystery.

That few attempt to fathom.

That few attempt to truly discover.

Few.

But some.

Some who retain some connection, some spark of that infinite, within them.

Some.

The man emerged, from the distance.

He had been monitoring its journey.

Monitoring from a hidden laboratory not far from here.

He is tall and lanky. With a dark, thick, thatch of hair upon his head. A kind face, doe brown eyes and a heavy mustache.

He was led to a short distance from the object by the Evenki hunters of the area, but once they reached a certain point, the point where his instruments began to react, they instinctively refused to go any further. Fearing what they called "the Valleymen" who are believed to be haunting the area.

And so, he continued alone, despite their warnings and protestations.

He continued. Knowing. Knowing what he could encounter. Knowing what he might.

What he believed would be revealed.

And when he sees the wreckage across the wilderness.

He sees the fallen object.

He can only speculate how far it has traveled.

He wonders how much it is connected to the other object he has discovered.

To the signals he's been getting.

Trying to decipher.

From the object. The black object. He has heard from his machines. That he has seen in his telescope.

That he has called, been compelled to call, The Black Knight.

And so, this man wonders if this fallen star is somehow of the same origin as the other object, which remains in its orbit above them.

There is something different about it. Very different. From the other meteors he has traced, that he has seen, that he has collected.

So, he collects samples. Collects evidence. Takes readings. Measurements.

And watches, and measures, with arcane instruments, as the energy remnants of this comet have continued to branch out, a web, spreading out across the distance. He feels as it runs through him, as he stands at the nexus of it. He feels no fear. Only an overwhelming sense of love. Of being. Of connection.

And when he has completed his initial tests, when he has fulfilled his initial mission, Nikola Tesla leaves this place, this vast area of wreckage, behind.

It will not be his final journey to this spot.

Nor will he be the last to visit it.

And as he leaves, he looks up, to the massive moon hovering brightly above, at the cusp of night.

A jewel with tales to tell, in a sky full of secrets.

Secrets he hopes to discover.

# TWENTY-TWO

## Hollywood, California

## 1968

The dusk rolled in, musky and oppressive, like a weight to the chest. The sun's light was dying slowly, bleeding out in rusted flame, but the darkening indigo pool drowning it offered little respite from the heat.

Frank Case had arrived unexpectedly.

He knew the bearded man was home, that much the man knew.

How much more he knew, the man was not sure.

"Frank," he said, as he opened the door, with forced cordiality.

Case merely nodded, gestured to the man, then moved without invitation to the back of the house, where he slid the large glass doors to the side and took a spot facing out over the city falling to night in the distance.

Case sat outside. He seemed cool, untouchable, completely comfortable despite the heat, despite being dressed in a crisp, tight black suit, black thin tie, white shirt. His greying hair was close-cropped and stylish, his face tanned and youthful.

A few moments later, the bearded man walked outside, handed Case a drink. Case looked it over a second, then nodded a thank you.

"You don't have to worry, I wouldn't poison you," the bearded man said, with a halted, uncomfortable chuckle.

"I know you wouldn't," Case said, with a smile. "You wouldn't want to deal with anyone who would follow me."

The bearded man nodded, and sat, uncomfortably. He was dressed in loose, off-white linen pants and a white linen shirt, opened to the middle of his chest, revealing golden chains from which a range of charms hung. He was a rounded man, heavy-set, tanned, with long, dark, wiry hair and a thick beard, each speckled with strings of gray. He wore small, circular, silver-rimmed glasses over his prominent nose and breathed heavily in the humid air, sweating in the late California summer.

They sat in silence. On an elaborately crafted deck. Beautiful foliage and brilliant glasswork about them, catching the fading light.

The sound of the city and the muted howls of coyotes rolled up the valley towards them, but as it had since the second man arrived, silence reigned, and they sat, outside of the presence of two other men in identical dark suits and glasses who had somehow slipped into the house behind them, unnoticed until now by the bearded man.

The other two men stood sentinel inside, while Case and the bearded man remained outside, beyond the glass doors, where they could speak freely.

The bearded man perched, chunky and disheveled, his nervous, ponderous gaze peering through the slight clear circles. Case sat casually, a thin knife, immaculately tailored and cut from his hair to his jaw to the dark suit which held him like a sheathe.

The man in white broke the silence.

"This is about the film," he said.

The man in black nodded. "In part."

"You are unhappy with it?"

"Not with it."

"With me?"

Case was silent.

The man's heart began to beat quickly. He wiped the sweat from his brow. He took a deep breath. Collected himself.

"One request?" the man in white said.

The man in black gestured and nodded.

"Can you make it look like an overdose rather than a suicide? My family . . ."

The man in black stopped him, shook his head slightly. "If we were going to kill you, you would be dead already."

The man in white lightened, leaned back in his chair.

"I liked the movie," Case said. "Capulet liked the movie. It will do exactly what we want it to do."

A quizzical look drew upon the face of the man in white.

"Is this about . . . the other project? The first project?"

Case was silent.

The man in white took a large drink.

Case was cold in his response. "You really shouldn't drink so much."

The man in white looked at Case, quizzically.

Case leaned forward and his eyes pierced the man in white's gaze.

"You really . . . should not . . . drink so much."

The man in white's gaze turned away sheepishly and his chin buried into his chest.

"Is there something that . . . you seemed very pleased when I had finished . . ."

Case looked at him squarely.

"We know."

"Know?"

Case shook his head slowly, disappointed.

"I like you, Stanley," Case said. "I appreciate your work, not just for Capulet, but as an artist."

"Thank you."

"We knew things about you that you didn't even know about yourself before we even approached you," the man in black said. "We knew exactly how you would react to the first project, to all of the information we gave you, to all of the things you now know, and we knew where it would lead you, and where we would lead you."

"Where you would lead me?"

The man in black leaned back in his chair.

"Capulet knows all."

The man in white shifted uncomfortably.

"Are you . . . going to . . ."

"No, again, as I said, we are not going to kill you," the man in black said, then leaned forward. "But we will have to, unfortunately, eliminate the two you have mistakenly told."

"Two?"

"We have no qualms with the third, he is already ours," the man in black said.

"Capulet . . ." the man in white whispered, as the picture of a friend, of one he thought a friend, appeared in his mind, and he faded in his chair, his hand wringing at his furrowing brow.

"How do you think he knew so much?" the man in black said. "His stories . . . he knew . . . about Huxley, Orwell . . . the first mission . . . the merchandise? The Knight? All of these conspiracy theorists popping up . . . did you not think some of them might be ours?"

The man in white, embarrassed at his foolishness, his face reddened and withering, looked up.

"Why? Why hide it? This is a new era, look around us. If people knew, the people who see, who see these things, who connect the puzzle, don't you believe . . ."

"You are incredibly naïve."

"I am hopeful," the man in white replied. "I believe . . ."

The man in black interrupted him sternly.

"We don't believe," he said. "We know. That's our job. To know."

"But . . ."

"You read Brookings," Case said. "We were quite clear."

"But, Frank . . . you're a good man, I know . . ."

Case finished his drink and stood up.

"I'm sorry, but this is how it has to be," Case said.

"But . . ." the man in white began, softly, but his voice betrayed his surrender.

"You won't be there, there will be no way of connecting you to it," Case said. "We have your next project. You will begin your next project. Then you will not hear from us for a long while, until we need you again."

The man in white began to sob, quietly.

"I didn't want to have to do it this way," the man in black said.

"Frank . . . I know you're a good . . ." the man in white began.

"Repeat after me," the man in black commanded.

"Can't you . . ."

"Repeat. After. Me."

The man in white broke down for a few seconds, then collected himself, took a deep breath, sat up, and looked forward.

The man in black paused a moment, softened his gaze, sighed.

"I'm sorry, Stan, I respect you. That's why you're not dead. That's why I brought you in when Pollux just wanted you gone after the first project. I saw the potential in you, I saw how we could help each other, and I liked your work," Case said. "But everyone is just a piece on the board. Even me."

The man in white looked up at him.

"One more, and then you'll be on your own for a while," the man in black said. "But if the cracks appear, you know what to do. Or we will. And I don't want to do that."

The man in white nodded, looked up at the other man.

"I liked the film," Case said, placing his hand on the other man's shoulder. "Very much."

The man in white gave him a slight smile.

The man in black returned his salutation, then went steely again and removed his hand from his shoulder, crossing his arms across his chest.

"Repeat after me," Case said.

The man in white sat upright, took a deep breath, curled his hands into fists.

"Repeat . . . after me," Case repeated, in a calm tone.

And his gaze pierced forward towards the other man.

The man in white relaxed, surrendered.

"Magician," the man in black began.

"Magician," the man in white replied.

"Kappa."

"Kappa."

"Umbrella."

"Umbrella."

The words continued, as the night fell about them, and their voices became drowned by the growing howls and the symphonies of the black of space.

Until Case was done.

And he left.

Hoping he wouldn't have to return.

But knowing he probably would.

# TWENTY-THREE

## Airspace over Arizona

## 2042


The rose, rust, sienna and gold of the desert stretched out before the hovercraft as it neared its destination. Bastian and Zinesha growing tense as it loomed. Both felt a strange sense of trepidation, but neither acknowledged it.

"So, what happened?" Zinesha asked, fidgeting. "Were the Annunaki all evil? How were they defeated?"

"Not all were evil," Bastian said. "No beings are all truly evil. Like humanity, some are good, some not. The Annunaki interbred with humans. For reasons good and ill. Some fell in love. Some merely ravaged those they thought beneath them. Both created armies of hybrid beings. On the side of the

Demiurge, espousing cruelty and subjugation of humanity, forcing them to obedience, were the Nephilim. On the side of the Elohim, the Watchers, who urged neutrality or helping humanity evolve, were the Magi. Both were half-Annunaki, half-human warriors. Eventually, through hundreds of years of battle, the Magi and those Annunaki on their side, the Elohim, that humanity called the Watchers, were triumphant over the Demiurge."

"How did they finally defeat them?"

"The Elohim imprisoned the bodies of the Demiurge within sarcophagi that acted as dimensional prisons, keeping them locked between dimensional planes. They stripped their power from them and contained it within the oculus stones and hid both the sarcophagi and the gems in various locations between the two worlds."

"Two?"

"Here, and the original world they colonized before coming to earth," Bastian said. "Mars."

"So, they were the original Martians."

"We all were."

Zinesha went silent, processing what she had heard, before venturing into the conversation again.

"So, if their bodies and their power are contained, how are they still a threat?"

"The bodies of the Demiurge were trapped in the sarcophagi, but regardless of the condition of any being's body, its soul can travel beyond it. The souls of the Demiurge were able to travel through the dimensional portals and wander the planet," Bastian said. "They would be able to possess human or animal forms, but neither could hold them for very long because neither were biologically capable of containing the souls of a higher evolutionary being. And so, they would wander from being to being, possessing those sacrificed to them through blood and ritual, or those who offered themselves foolishly, thinking it would increase their own power."

"Why didn't they go back to their own planet and find bodies there?" Zinesha asked.

"The souls weren't able to escape this world because of two satellites, sent by the Annunaki millennia ago, which keep them, and other spirits of the Elohim and Demiurge, chained to this planet and the nearby dimensional planes. One of the satellites, the Black Knight, was severely damaged by the Thule, the Nazi occult who were trying to bring back the Demiurge during World War II to help them conquer the planet. Since then, over the last 100 years, the Black Knight has been slowly dying, and now is almost near its end. And as it has slowly decayed, the dimensional gates it kept tight around this planet have been disintegrating, allowing the spirits of the Demiurge to possess and use the bodies of others sometimes against their will to use them to find their sarcophagi, their oculus stones, so that they can be united, and can once more rule this planet."

"So why don't people know this?" Zinesha said. "I mean, there are 10 billion people in the world, plus the Magi and Sikari and all of the military, with nuclear weapons and everything. You would think by now they would be able to defeat them."

"Possibly, but not all are against the Demiurge," Bastian said. "And some don't even acknowledge their existence. Nor even ours."

"But how can you not?"

"From the time you are born you are programmed, programmed to think a certain way, to think that this is plausible, and this is not. Information is framed, as fact, as fiction, as entertainment, as speculation, as history, as belief. Investigation and information are forbidden and seen as strange and verboten. And so, the bias is created, the prison bars welded around the minds of society."

Zinesha slunk back into her seat.

"You know the easiest way to imprison someone?" Bastian said. "Let them believe they are free."

"So, you said the Magi and the Elohim return," Zinesha said, timidly, "can humans return as well?"

"Some, yes," Bastian said. "The Magi have a long lineage, going back thousands of years. And in Magi and humans, in all beings, spirits never die. And, yes, some return, drawn to those they once held dear. Some return to protect the world they once called home."

She looked at Zinesha as she began guiding the hovercraft down, as they pulled within a few miles of the Sikari outpost.

"Or," Bastian said, "they return, drawn to those who are their descendants. To those they loved. And love."

"So," Zinesha said, "what's going to happen?"

"We shall see," Bastian said. "The chess pieces are being put on the board. And we don't have many left."

It was then she saw the first signs of the wreckage. The slight glow emitting from the Sikari compound.

Zinesha could tell by the look on Bastian's face that something was wrong.

"What is it?"

"They got here first."

"Who?"

Their craft jolted as it was caught in a beam of light from above. A magnetic lock, freezing their ship and slowly drawing them upward, upward, into the waiting belly of a huge, silver, triangular craft.

Bastian looked up. She did not recognize the craft. Unusual. Very unusual.

But it was definitely not Thule.

Zinesha scuttled about her seat, looking up, nervous.

"Who is it?"

"I . . . don't know."

"You don't know. You. That's reassuring."

"Don't worry," Bastian said. "If they wanted to kill us, they would've shot us out of the sky."

"You mean if they wanted to kill us right away," Zinesha said. "As opposed to torturing us or killing us slowly."

"Such an optimist you are," Bastian said. "I thought you were raised by hippies?"

"I was raised by them, I didn't say I was one."

"Fair enough."

"So, what do we do?" Zinesha said.

"Nothing now," Bastian said. "But wait to see what fresh hell or heaven, what friend or foe, waits in store for us."

# TWENTY-FOUR

**New York City**

**2042**

From the panoramic view of his penthouse high above the city, the Arimathean looked down, down upon the golden grid, upon the frantic streets, and as he did, it seemed as if time overlapped and moved in slow motion.

He remembered when he had first walked upon these lands, hundreds of years past. He had wanted to escape, far away from the world he had traveled. The wars he had fought. The people he had lost.

He had discovered a map. One which had been hidden from him. From all. One which had been part of an ancient history those in power had tried to destroy or keep in secret.

He landed upon this soil. Observed the natives from afar. Living off the land. In unison with nature. He watched them. Then approached them, found a way to communicate, to show he was not a threat, and he found them to be welcoming, innocent in many ways, far different from those he had encountered in the many centuries prior.

And so, he remained, for many years, many decades, in this land.

He remembered, fondly, a much simpler time. When he laid upon his back in seas of green grass and watched the clouds drift above him as children told stories to their mothers about them.

He wandered the whole of this land. Over the rushing rivers and sanguine lakes, the mountains, and canyons austere and deathly quiet, to the ocean, vast beyond here.

And then, he sailed once more, to other lands, beyond this one.

He returned centuries later, again.

After the Europeans had settled.

He returned to find himself no longer embraced, but feared.

Once more, he retreated, seeking solace. Seeking peace.

But finding none.

And so, he returned once more to these lands, no longer a man apart, drifting, but one who strode to conquer. Not with sword, not with steel, but with intellect and cunning.

One who found distance, and peace.

Before once more being dragged back, into war.

Always, echoing back, into battle.

He noticed just how much civilization had changed in the last two millennia, and it did not move him. It disgusted him. The disease of greed. Willful ignorance. Unrepentant cruelty.

There were magnificent and beautiful aspects to humanity, he knew.

But all too often they were crushed, destroyed, needlessly.

By delusion. By greed. By fear. By evil.

In many ways, perhaps, he thought, civilization had not changed much at all.

And that darkened him even more.

He watched as people walked through the grid, with advertising holograms floating above their body parts, miniature chips tattooed just beneath their skin and rented out to the highest bidder. He knew that their ID chips interacted with these "willful" tattoos, made the hosts more subservient to the tech's commercial whims as the ad chips manipulated their brainwaves through magnetic fields, the same way the ID chips did.

He knew those same chips emitted the magnetic waves that rendered almost all humanity sterile – all but those that fell beneath the freak less than one percent who were immune or whose systems had mutated beyond the magnetic current – until they could pass a government-administered series of tests in applying for a license to have children. And even then, every time they wished to breed, they had to pass the same series of tests, to prove themselves worthy of reproduction in a world of untold billions. Untold billions whose unchecked reproduction had pushed the world to the brink, pushed humanity to the edge of self-extinction, and whose depravity and irresponsibility had led the Arimathean to create the technology within the chips, to control humanity and prevent its virus from spreading any more upon the planet.

He looked at the hired lots where the Tubeway fields spread out, vast armies of armored cars that acted as not only transport and protection to the highest bidder, but as homes to those within them, nomads who used public bathing facilities when they bathed at all, who ate what they could scrounge or gather at drive-through restaurants from day-to-day, who were usually migrant workers. Sometimes the Tubeways remained unmoved, stuck and rusted, in the fields, as their occupants arrived and left them day after day in a pathetic march of basic existence, until they would remain sentinel, and an odor would emit from them, announcing they had become tombstones to the decaying and dead within.

He looked at this world, the world he had seen decay, become poisoned by its own greed, hatred, ignorance, and stupidity. The world he had spent most his life trying to save.

The world he now could not wait to be destroyed, to release him from his prison.

The secret scriptures, set far away within the caves, never released to the masses, told that when the Christ energy next returned to earth, when it next fully manifested a human, it would act as a destructive force, the exact translation said.

And so, as the Arimathean grew increasingly disgusted with humanity, and as he faced each tragedy and each disappointment increasingly alone, he pored over the information he obtained and dissected the planet and the universe for the signs that the Christ's return was near.

Until he finally began to find them.

And so, he knew, did his enemies.

Their activities became even more brazen, even more desperate, even more diabolical.

And even as he tried to stop them, he eventually realized he couldn't stop them all.

Nor, perhaps, was he meant to.

For if the Christ was meant to return as destroyer, as re-creator, perhaps, perhaps, his enemies, whose goal seemed to wipe the slate clean as well, to destroy all that came before, were more aligned with his own desires, his own objectives, than his allies.

Perhaps.

And perhaps, he would engage them to find out.

Once he had taken control, it became easy to master the paradigm. Problem, reaction, solution. Have the end solution in mind. Create the problem that would lead the people to demand it. Have the reaction, the conduit to the final solution, already in place in the shadows, waiting for the populace to demand it.

It had become child's play. Swing the pendulum in either direction too far and people would demand equilibrium.

He had allowed the city to become a cesspool, not too long ago. Most drugs had become legal, ostensibly for monetary reasons, but in truth, to placate part of the populace and to make another part more easily driven to anger, for once a man was angry, he was easier to control.

It was a volatile situation, just ripe for a revolution. And, soon enough, it arrived. The poor were broken to the point where they had nothing to lose, and when they had passed that point, the riots and the killings began. Computer hackings and redistribution of wealth became epidemic. Rampages through wealthy neighborhoods were commonplace. The police, many of whom had come from the lower classes to begin with, were hardly sympathetic to the plight of the ultra-rich, most of whom had worked to put them out of work or on lower wages, hiring their own private security firms to guard them.

But the problem with mercenaries, as the rich soon learned, is that their loyalties were easily swayed. They were master to only themselves, and their wallets.

The Arimathean worked through his proxies to bribe and thwart security, allowing the wealthy to be decimated, killed, or pillaged, until most of the money had become ostensibly dispersed throughout the population, into millions of different companies. Millions of companies, but with one thing in common: Each of them having a tie, most clandestine, to a secret corporation, its strings held by the Arimathean.

And then when the strings pulled too tightly, and chaos beckoned, the Arimathean was there to offer the perfect solutions. Small drone robots began patrolling neighborhoods, because robots couldn't be bribed or controlled. They were impartial, connected to a master system that could not be hacked, in part because those with the knowledge of doing so were found and eliminated. And, of course, microchipping for the population.

And this way, too, the Arimathean could keep track of not only the population, but the change in population, and the number of unauthorized births, because he knew that only one thing could override the frequency, and that was the one power that was beyond him.

He had seen the rise in unauthorized conceptions, seen the steady growth, and he knew that eventually one would arise that was different. Unable to be negated. And he also knew that if that one, that chosen one, was conceived by a woman on his grid, someone who was chipped, he would be able to locate her, and would know that finally, the Christ would be arriving.

Arriving to finally end his guardianship of this planet.

Arriving to finally allow him peace.

The door to his office opened behind him and the Arimathean turned to see his son, Vanth, with the one he had been sent to retrieve.

One who was once a friend.

No longer.

Dorin Xerxes.

"Hello, my friend," Xerxes said. "It is, good, to see you again."

"I wish I could say the same," the Arimathean said.

Vanth led Xerxes over to the Arimathean, looming behind him.

"I have no patience, Dorin, it has long left me," the Arimathean said, "So please do not lie to me and waste both our time. I know you have certain information I need, and I would prefer not to have to torture you to get it."

"I don't know . . ." Xerxes began.

The Arimathean slammed his fist upon the marble table in front of him.

"Do not lie to me!" the Arimathean raged at him.

Xerxes cowered as the immortal warrior loomed over him, his face red and boiling with rage.

"You have betrayed me, again," the Arimathean said, through gritted teeth.

"No," Xerxes plead.

"And now I won't bother asking you," the Arimathean said, "I'll take what I need."

The Arimathean looked full into his face with hatred. Xerxes knew he was doomed. He began to tear up, to plead.

The Arimathean paid no heed to his begging. Xerxes shut his eyes tightly, but the Arimathean's mind was already in his, and he felt its icy tendrils snaking through his brain, quickly locating the information he needed.

And . . . more than he wanted to know. A dark secret Xerxes had kept from him. One which stunned even the Arimathean at its depravity.

The Arimathean's face grew red, his teeth gritted with anger, and his rage seethed, tearing into Xerxes' mind, painfully, like barbed wire being slashed across Xerxes' brain.

"I trusted you," the Arimathean said. "You . . . you . . . "

"No, please," Xerxes plead, "I had no choice, they threatened me, I, they offered me the ultimate blessing, escape from death . . ."

"It is no blessing!" the Arimathean erupted, his hand grasping Xerxes throat. "It is the ultimate curse. And one you shall never know!"

Xerxes' hands went to his neck, to try to struggle free, but the Arimathean's iron grasp remained and tightened about his windpipe as he gasped and choked.

"You . . . helped them, you killed my wives, my children, to keep me as a weapon for your wars," the Arimathean said. "You knew if I lost them, if I lost all, I would have nothing to live for, nothing but battle, nothing but to live as a weapon for your pathetic struggles, your poisonous wars! You killed them! All but the two, the only two, to survive, and they only did so because of the one you and your order had painted as my enemy. But you . . . you . . . were the only serpent I needed to beware."

The Arimathean's eyes burned with hatred, with pain, with vengeance.

"You will have no escape from death," the Arimathean said. "Be grateful I bring it swiftly to you. For that is the only concession you deserve from me."

And with those words, his hand closed and crushed Xerxes neck, the body collapsing in the Arimathean's grasp, as he dropped it dead to the ground.

"I know exactly where they are," the Arimathean said bitterly. "And I know exactly the cost to obtain them."

He nodded to Vanth. Their minds merged, and within his son's mind, images flashed.

Vanth nodded.

He looked to the dead body upon the carpet.

"Should I dispose of it?"

"No need," the Arimathean said, and with a thought from him, Xerxes' body erupted in flame. "He is gone. As those who helped him will soon be as well."

# TWENTY-FIVE

## New York City

## 2042

For a week, the city was awash in blood.

Explosions rocked buildings within the elites' zone, creating a lockdown and temporary curfew which was almost superfluous, since most fled within before night's fall, for fear of death in the seemingly random slayings.

But they were hardly random.

Most, were hardly random.

Most were conducted with surgical precision.

As Vanth the Destroyer laid waste to those who dared to poison the Silent Hand from within. Who had turned it against the one who had kept it alive for millennia.

Nearly half of its members were killed, most in their sleep, as the Destroyer found them.

Enclaves were bombed, hollowed out, bodies dismembered and displayed for the media drones to find.

To send a very clear message to those who may have thought of betrayal.

At any point.

By week's end, the bloodbath was at its end.

And all were at bowed knee.

To the one who ruled them unquestionably.

However, within the realm of the massacre came a handful of fluke explosions and killings.

The drones showed them quite clearly.

A shaded figure.

Acting in self-defense.

Shambling his way through the city, seemingly without goal, without aim.

Falling prey to the packs, the throngs of the wild, those seeking to slay him, or worse, but instead finding their fate, finding their own deaths at his hand.

And in each case, an incredible eruption of energy, of magnetic power, that registered upon the instruments, the satellites.

At first, they seemed random.

Then, suspect.

And then, the Arimathean realized who it was.

And so, he sent Vanth to bring the man forth.

To use their magicks, to calm and reassure him, if necessary.

To find this wild being who had scythed such a jagged path across his city.

And who had, in his wake, also likely become visible to others as well.

Vanth found the man holed up in a Tubeway station.

Among a handful of others.

Living beside two dead within a rusted vault.

He approached him, calmly, hoping to avoid battle.

He did.

The minute he was within reach, the man calmed.

Vanth looked into his eyes.

Dark purple and silver, bright as gems upon his deep ebon skin.

And he looked into Vanth's eyes.

So familiar.

Like those he had seen before.

Vanth reached out to him, and an energy flared between them.

Vanth spoke calmly to him.

"Balthazar . . ."

And all at once, it returned to the man.

A whirlwind, a torrent of information, tearing through the mind of the reincarnated Magi.

And tears came to his eyes.

And he embraced the son of one he once fought beside.

One he once called friend.

And one he had hoped to see again.

And would.

Once more.

After so many years.

So many centuries.

He was back on earth.

A Magi reborn.

But what had he returned to face?

# TWENTY-SIX

## Dulce, New Mexico

## 2042

Deep below the desert, beneath a scalding, burned earth mountain range, and tons of harsh, desolate rock and sand, were clandestine levels of glimmering steel. Guarded by hundreds of heavily armed soldiers, clad in the ebon and red uniforms of the top-secret installation.

Each level required a separate pass code and hand and retinal scan which admitted fewer people the further down it plunged, into the bowels of the earth.

At the lowest level, three figures watched behind a foot of clear plexiglass shield as blue lightning flashed within a massive circular room.

Along the walls of the room, strapped to stainless steel slabs decorated with intricate sigils in an ancient language, older than the recorded history of humanity, were the thirty-three humans they had abducted and kept imprisoned for this moment. Each had been located through the grid, through the DNA data base, and all were confirmed to have the genetic code needed to supply the requisite power to reincarnate the Demiurge. They were naked and dead, occult symbols carved upon their flesh, bled out and held in stasis, having been abducted and subjected to arcane rituals since their captivity began, to calibrate their vibratory status, to ready their blood, for the ritual.

For the raising of the body in the sarcophagus to which they, and the others, were attached.

The sarcophagus which had been imbued with the blood and life force of hundreds before them now discarded.

One of the only sarcophagi remaining.

One of the nine Tombs of the Demiurge.

Found by the Thule.

For decades, they had searched the world for the relics, the Centauri stones, containing the power of the Demiurge, but had not located them. The Silent Hand, the Sikari, the Vendari, Capulet, whichever group had them hidden, had managed to keep the stones from them.

Some of the other relics, or at least those that hadn't been destroyed by Capulet, had been located. Including the Codex of the Elohim, which had enabled the Thule to decipher the spell which would reanimate the bodies in the sarcophagi, the shells of the Demiurge, the multidimensional beings which had once ruled the earth, which many of the humans had worshipped as gods.

During the second world war, the Nazis had managed, through technological and occult means, to disable one of the ancient alien satellites which had been sent to guard the earth. The rift ripped in the dimensions caused by the crippling of the Black Knight satellite had allowed a few of the stronger spirits of the Nephilim to re-enter the earthen dimension.

Along with the spirit of their leader.

The one called The Babylonian.

However, while their spirits had returned, they remained disembodied. The Babylonian's energy, and the energy of the other Nephilim, was too powerful to be contained within human bodies, and so they quickly burned through human hosts. Genetic engineering utilizing ancient DNA found in recovered Nephilim bones as well as the DNA of select Nazis was conducted in clandestine laboratories in South America and built the Nephilim a host of different shells.

Until the sarcophagi could be located.

The first four sarcophagi that had been found, starting with the first two located during World War II, had been destroyed. The Sarcophagus of Set in Hiroshima. The Sarcophagus of Tezcatl in Nagasaki. The Sarcophagus of Ninjursag in Iraq. The Sarcophagus of Enlil, destroyed in flight, en route from the moon.

All destroyed through nuclear annihilation, by the multinational secret society, Capulet.

The location of two sarcophagi remained unknown. The sarcophagi of Tiamat and Dahaka.

The seventh sarcophagus had been found in a barren, icy wasteland in the old Soviet Union in the mid- '80s, during the cold war, and led to the reanimation of its occupant.

Shernihaza. Leader of the Nephilim.

The black magick societies that reanimated him sought to use him as an ultimate weapon, to control him.

Much to their regret.

Which was as short lived as they were once the body was brought back to life.

The sarcophagus of the Babylonian, a being once known as Anu, was found in Iraq in 1991. It was transported through various occult channels and exchanged hands repeatedly before finally being taken by the shadow elements of the U.S. government and brought to a facility in Groom Lake, Nevada.

In defiance of the Order of Capulet to destroy all relics and sarcophagi recovered, for the safety of humanity, the U.S. shadow government, like the Russians, attempted to resurrect the being as a weapon.

And, like the Russians, they did not live long to fully regret it.

It wasn't long until Shernihaza joined The Babylonian with the New Reich in Antarctica, engineering an army of Reichtarg Nephilim clones, and plotting how they would once more conquer this world.

The humans had become powerful, and there were other beings, which the Demiurge needed to eliminate, before they could rule.

And so, they plotted to conquer.

Beginning with the location and destruction of all reincarnated Magi, as well as the ultimate destruction of those descended from the Magi.

Along with the location and destruction of any child that may emerge containing the genetic code to harness the energy of the Christos.

As well as the location and reincarnation of the last of their trinity of evil.

The sarcophagus of whom they located on Mars.

Which was brought back with the crew of the Atlantis.

And which was now feeding on the crew of the Atlantis.

Their life energies were filtered through an intricate system of tubes, into the item they had brought back from their expedition to Mars. An ancient, golden sarcophagus decorated with ornate, powerful gems and drawn with an elaborate golden mural, a grotesque depiction of the disgusting creature within.

The artifact had been known of only by the ancients, secret societies formed by the elite bloodlines of the twin planets. Knowledge passed down through generations. Knowledge originated by those beings who had created the sarcophagus and who had captured and imprisoned the being locked within it.

The being locked within The Womb of the Demiurge.

A being whose demonic spirit and fetid resonance had been a petulance, a disease, upon humanity for millennia. Even outside its body, it had continued to be a force for evil within the world, deceiving countless humans and other beings into acting as its host, to further its malevolence and destruction.

But now, its original shell recovered, it would no longer need weak human hosts.

Now it would regain its own throne of power.

Slowly, an awful, moaning shriek began to fill the room as the sarcophagus began to glow, glow a bright red.

"It is ready," the tall man in the lab coat and thin steel glasses said.

The being next to him, Shernihaza, smirked, as his eyes grew crimson and a growing scent of Sulphur began to engulf his body.

And behind them both, a third figure, clad in shadow, watched.

The one who had engineered the mission.

The one who had orchestrated the ritual.

The one who had orchestrated a similar ritual beneath the last blood moon, for himself, to finally be enthroned within his own ancient shell, now joined with its Centauri stone to regain its ultimate power.

The one known as The Babylonian.

As the ritual within the room neared its end, The Babylonian strode to the thick, plexiglass and steel door leading to the sarcophagus room. He tapped in a code to the key pad next to it, placed his hand over a scanner that read his handprint, and watched as the door slowly opened to him.

He walked in, to stand six feet in front of the sarcophagus. He raised his hand, to reveal a strange silver and crimson gemmed object wrapped around his fist, and as he did, the sarcophagus trembled.

The Centauri stone of the being within.

The Babylonian smiled widely as the sarcophagus opened, slowly, with an eerie green glow. The Babylonian motioned, and Shernihaza and the scientist followed him into the room, the scientist tentative, his face pocked by fear, Shernihaza smiling as his eyes burned with evil.

The sarcophagus opened wide, and an acrid fog emitted from it and dissipated with a horrible odor.

Within was a body, over seven feet tall, thin, and wiry, clad in a skin-tight silver suit made of liquid metal.

Its hands were crossed over its chest, its eyes closed.

But its countenance made even the scientist gasp.

He had seen pictures, even seen those of its ilk, but had never seen one so hideous.

Its skin was pale and sickly, scaled and slick. Its face reptilian, with a huge gash of a mouth teeming with rows of razor sharp teeth, and its head jagged with grotesque horns.

A burst of green light tore around the sarcophagus and into the body.

The Babylonian released the Centauri stone from his grasp and it levitated towards the being in the sarcophagus, lodging in its chest.

And with a barbed wire snaking of lightning about the sarcophagus and the stone, the two were conjoined.

And with a jolt, the being's eyes opened.

It gasped.

Opened its vicious mouth and spewed forth a viscous goo, then grasped for air, sucking it in through its hideous maw, its razor-sharp teeth and thin reptilian tongue.

And once more, it resided within its original body, and it emerged from its sarcophagus, with a devious cackle.

The being's eyes opened wide, turned an opaque white, then a bright red, the body filled with life. Malevolent life. And the reptilian strode, with a sickening smile, from its centuries-long prison, and onto the steel, back, back, again, to this planet, back to earth, alien flesh and demonic soul entwined with violent power, seeking to subjugate, and destroy.

Destroy, and conquer.

At the side of the one standing before him, which had not long before emerged from its own sarcophagus.

The Babylonian.

The reptilian being smiled, a razor's cut of a smile, all grotesque teeth and glowing crimson slits of eyes.

"So...." The reptilian hissed, "we meet again... brother."

"Yes, we do," the Babylonian smirked. "Satanus."

The reptilian raised its arms and gazed upon its body, and a grin crossed its disgusting face.

"Ahhhh, my favorite throne, mine once again," Satanus hissed. "How I have missed this one made for me to stride upon these twin worlds."

Satanus looked at the other two beings with he and The Babylonian. He smiled deviously at Shernihaza, and then, wickedly at the scientist.

The human's face was a mask of fear, his heart pounding in his chest, his blood tearing through his veins.

"Is this one another of the Demiurge? Does he carry its blood or its poison upon his soul?" Satanus said.

"Neither," The Babylonian said.

"Then what is he for?" Satanus hissed, sneering at the scientist.

The Babylonian's eyes narrowed and he smiled.

"Well," The Babylonian said, "After such a long trip, I thought you might be hungry."

Satanus grinned, then savagely attacked the human.

The scientist's screams echoed through the chamber as the fangs of Satanus tore into him.

The Babylonian and Shernihaza looked upon the slaughter and laughed.

"Soon the others shall join us," the Babylonian smiled. "This entire world shall be little more than a blood feast for us to harvest upon once more, and no one, not the Magi nor the traitor who betrayed and helped imprison us, will stand in our way."

# TWENTY-SEVEN

## New York City

## 2015

His eyes were burnt and red.

His face remained a mask of suffering.

His stoic features shaken, his face raw and unshaven.

As much as he tried, he could not control his sobbing, his heart shattered and cold.

Cold as her hand, in his.

She remained in the bed.

Silent.

Still.

Unbreathing.

And he let her go. Unclasped his hand from hers and placed her delicate porcelain fingers upon her chest.

He kissed her face. Kissed her lips. His tears falling on to her face.

And then turned away, away from her.

For he had no choice.

He turned.

To the other two, tiny beds in the room.

The beds in which their twin three-year-old children lay dying.

Dying from the same affliction as their mother.

The odds of all three contracting it were infinitely small, the doctors had said.

And somewhere, deep inside of him, he wondered if somehow it was because of him. Some mutation of his genes over the centuries. Some anomaly of his immune system that allowed him to carry it without lethal effect to himself. Some way in which he had been the cause of their suffering. The cause of her death.

The cause of his children's inevitable deaths.

The doctors did their best. They were amazed she had lasted long as she did, for as much pain as she struggled through. This dark beast drowning her, until it eventually took her.

And now, he, Josephus, was forced, again, to sit helplessly by and watch.

Watch again, as he had been, as his children succumbed to it. As he watched the darkness overcome them, until they too would drown in its abyss, and they, like so many others he had loved, would leave him, and become faded memories of those he had once been able to love, to hold, to carry near.

They would not survive the night, the doctors said.

He watched them both, feverish and in pain, dulled with sedatives, and his face filled once more with agony, his eyes stinging with tears.

His right hand holding the small hand of his son, Vanth. Still stoic, breathing heavily, his face a closed fist of concentration, bright crimson and drenched in sweat.

His left hand holding the tiny hand of his daughter, Bastian. Calming her slightly as she quaked and struggled, her face twisted in pain.

He used all his power.

All his strength.

Every bit of his magicks, his abilities, to keep all three of them alive as long as he could.

But he could feel them slipping, slipping from his hands.

The same as she had.

Within his heart, he had prayed, so many times, only to find those prayers unanswered. Only to find himself alone once more.

But still, he allowed himself to do so again.

To send a plea out to the universe.

For something.

Someone.

Anyone to help him.

And then, faintly, outside the door, he heard the deep tones of a familiar voice. One he had not heard in decades. One which he had ignored. Avoided. Not wanted to hear.

Until now.

The words of someone he had known for centuries.

Whose last words to him, decades before, echoed in his mind.

And which he was now thankful for.

As he was now thankful.

For a prayer miraculously answered.

Weeks later, his children, remarkably healed, would accompany him, as they laid their mother to rest.

And as always, from that day forward, his children remained, close to him, almost always by his side.

And he would remember.

Remember that night.

The night they had been pulled from death.

Would remember the note that had been delivered to him shortly after they returned home.

Delivered with a small, dark box, covered in silver sigils and intricate patterns of velvet and onyx.

Would remember what was inside.

Remember what it meant.

And who had delivered it.

# TWENTY-EIGHT

## New York City

## 2042

The doors to the Arimathean's penthouse atrium opened and Vanth stepped aside, Balthazar behind him.

Vanth had brought the reincarnated Magi to the opulent multi-level complex and allowed him to dine, shower, and be dressed in fine clothing that was retrieved and delivered while Balthazar was preparing and relaxing.

Balthazar looked upon the massive, magnificent room looking out over the entirety of the city, the walls covered in glass high above this new world, and he was, for a moment, stunned at the evolution this world had undergone during his time apart from it.

And in the midst of the room, behind a herculean marble table covered with various screens and holographic buttons, stood a man, his back turned to Balthazar, looking out over the city.

The man he had once known.

Who he had once fought beside.

Who he had once called friend.

The Arimathean.

Balthazar smiled widely as he strode, slowly but surely, towards his fellow Magi.

The Arimathean turned, and greeted him with a wide smile, but one which seemed slightly distant, slightly pained.

Balthazar reached out, arms open, and they embraced.

"It is good to see you again, my friend," Balthazar said. "It has been far too long. Far too long."

The Arimathean slowly separated from him, holding him at arm's length.

"Have your accommodations been to your liking? I am sorry it took us so long to bring you here."

"They have been magnificent," Balthazar said. "I am grateful. Grateful to see you again."

"And I, you," the Arimathean said.

Balthazar looked out over the horizon, over the city.

"This world . . . it is . . . astonishing," Balthazar said. "So different from the earth I once knew."

"You have no idea," the Arimathean said. "No idea, how the years have gone. The things I have seen in this world."

"I am, sorry, my friend, I sense, great distress in you," Balthazar said, stepping back from him.

The Arimathean looked downward.

Behind them, the sound of a steel door opening sliced the air.

"And I, too, am sorry," the Arimathean said.

"But, for what?" Balthazar said.

"For this," the Arimathean said, looking at him, his face stony, his eyes cold.

Balthazar took two steps backward and froze. Around him erupted a massive blue force field torn by lightning, holding him motionless. His eyes were filled with shock, and, sadness.

"What . . . what are you doing?" Balthazar said to the Arimathean, surprised.

"What needs to be done," the Arimathean said.

And then, Balthazar heard the voice.

The voice from behind him.

One so familiar.

But which he had not heard, for many, many, centuries before.

But which he knew, all too well.

Enki.

"Hello, Balthazar," Enki said, his hand held up slightly, as his, Vanth's and the Arimathean's power held Balthazar captive within the aura of the Centauri stone. "I would say it's a pleasure to see you again, but I'm not quite sure it is."

Balthazar struggled to escape, but his efforts were futile.

Faced with the power of the three supernatural beings and the Centauri stone, he had no choice.

He was captive.

And as he looked out of the energy haloed around him, he saw it, enshrined in a small magnetic field upon the Arimathean's desk, surrounded by small, floating crystals of gold.

Saw it and realized, he had no choice.

But to face these three.

To face his fate.

He saw.

The black pearl.

# EPILOGUE

## Denver

## 2042

The woman gasped, limping, towards the sleek silver building, in the dark of night, its light a beacon in the midst of the dismal shading of the world around it.

She pounded on the door with blood on her hands, screaming for help.

The security guard scrambled from his perch to the door.

There was a moment, a moment, where she thought she saw the hint of a smile, the glint of something savage and sinister in his eyes. She saw it, when he first got a look at her. At her body, athletic and curved, her clothing ripped and revealing. At her face, sweaty and sleek with blood, looking as if she'd been beaten, as if she was running, looking for anyone to help her.

A moment. A brief moment.

And then, she saw it again, as he opened the door.

She was alone.

It was the thick of night.

He was alone.

"Help . . . help me . . ." she gasped, coughing.

She fell into him, and for a moment, she felt him grasp her, strangely tight, as if not wanting to let her go.

She pulled away from him. It took effort. He didn't want to let go.

"What happened?" he said.

"I was . . . attacked . . . raped . . . they . . ."

"There was more than one?"

She nodded, gasping, and her breathing became harsh, as if she was going to cry.

"Help me. . . please. . ." she said.

"Come in," the guard said. "Come with me."

"You'll help me?" she said.

"Yeah," the guard said, with a smirk in his voice.

And she knew.

She knew.

Their advance reconnaissance had been correct.

He walked to his station, told her to sit down. She sat, head bowed, her long, dark hair covering her face.

He reached behind the desk and she could hear clicking, as he flicked switches.

Turning the cameras off.

Turning the scanners off.

"Come with me," he said.

She stood up, and he grabbed her arm, held it tight, and began to lead her across the lobby.

"Where are you taking me?" she said.

"You'll see," he said, leading her towards the elevator, and pressing a code as lasers scanned his retina and the door slowly opened.

"Are you going to help me?" she said.

"I'm going to help you alright," he said, laughing sardonically.

Through her matted hair, she could see the red glow of the cameras had gone dark.

The elevator door closed behind them.

Once the two were enclosed in the space, he pulled her tightly to his body. His hands roamed her and he grabbed her tight.

"But first I'm going to help myself," he said, as his breath went hot on her cheek and his hands grabbed her body.

But they didn't get far.

Her hands clasped tight, in an iron grip, around his wrists.

"What the . . ." the guard said, shocked.

With a quick move, she headbutted his face, breaking his nose, sending a quick rivulet of blood down his chin onto his chest. He screamed out in pain.

He tried to grab her again, but his arms were locked in her grip.

With a rapid move, she whirled him around and was behind him, twisting his arm in a grotesque position and driving him to his knees.

"What are you doing?" he said through gritted teeth.

"You had the chance to help me," she said. "Now I'm helping myself."

"Helping yourself . . . to what?"

She ignored him, only tightening her grip as he grimaced and growled in pain.

Leaning her head to her shoulder, she clicked on the communicator embedded in her clothing.

"I'm in," she said. "Cameras are out."

She listened.

"Yeah, no problem."

She turned to the guard.

"You're going to open the front doors now."

"Like hell I am!"

With one jerk, she snapped his arm.

He fell to the floor screaming in pain, his broken arm fallen like a rag doll's at his side.

She grabbed the other arm and thrust it behind his back at the same disgusting angle.

"Ok, maybe you're not going to be able to now, but you're going to tell me how to," she said.

"Ok, ok!" he cried.

She dragged him up and made him open the elevator with his good hand.

Then she walked him over to the control console by the front door.

"The code."

The man looked back at her with a scowl.

"Sisyphus."

Holding tight to his arm, she pulled a device out of her pocket and punched the code in. Within the device was a holographic interface which locked onto any codes of the same nature within a 500-foot radius. While it could not crack encryption as sophisticated as that within this building, encryption which would instantly alert its owners if anyone dared to attempt a break, it could detect if the user's attempts were valid and allow them an unlimited number of attempts at decoding a security device.

"That's not it."

The security guard laughed.

"You're never going to get through, and even if you do, you won't get past security on the other levels," the man spat. "I'm just here for show."

She looked around, remembering all she had studied.

"Let it not be said I didn't give you the chance," she said.

"What's that supposed to mean?"

"Make peace with your god if you have one," she said.

"You don't scare me," he said. "There's no . . ."

With one swift move, she snapped his neck.

"You had your chance. My conscience is clear."

She tapped her communicator.

"Tanara in," Tanara said.

"Good job," the voice on the other end replied.

Tanara kneeled, placed her hand on the man's head. Did as she had been taught, years before. Entered the man's mind. It was much simpler than she thought it would be. The code had been right there, hovering from where he had recalled it, but refused to surrender it, just before she killed him. Along with the other codes she needed.

She took out a small laser blade from the black lace tight at the top of her stocking, around her thigh, and quickly removed the guard's eye from its ocular cavity.

She tapped in the code to the key by the front door. Used the eye to open the retinal scanner.

The door opened and in flooded a cadre of thirty-two Sikari, joining their leader.

"I have the codes," Tanara said.

"So, I see," one warrior said, nodding to the corpse on the floor.

"That's the choice he made," Tanara said, as they quickly moved to the elevator.

They had been casing the building for months, as soon as they had realized this was where the artifact had been housed.

Housed in a mundane laboratory, nothing special or heavily guarded.

A banal home for it, to deflect suspicion.

For centuries, the true artifact had been housed in Turin.

Until 1997.

The Vendari had staged an elaborate ruse, centered around a fake arson attempt and thwarted robbery, using a handful of dupes who had no idea they were mere pawns. It allowed the Vendari to make away with the original shroud and replace it with a replica.

In 2002 the Silent Hand stole it. Then again, in 2025, by the Thule. And once more five years later by the Vendari.

None of them had found what they were looking for. And with all three having lost interest, but not wanting to surrender it in case some evidence to the contrary arose later, the true shroud remained in hiding, eventually making its way to Denver, to be hidden away in an inconspicuous office building.

Only the Sikari knew the truth.

The cadre of Sikari split up, half of them into the elevator, the other half remaining on guard at the main floor.

They didn't have much time. Eventually someone would notice the cameras out. And while they had known this guard had a penchant for having visitors, and wanting privacy, they knew that if the cameras remained silent for too long, the Vendari would become suspicious.

They ascended to the floor. Door opened. Quickly, Tanara threw a sonic scrambler into the space, cutting all signals and cameras.

There were at least a dozen guards, blasters drawn, just inside the doors. But with lightning speed, the Sikari threw a handful of laser shuriken and they were quickly dispatched.

Tanara's eyes scanned the area, until finally finding what she sought.

And what was keeping her from it.

A half-dozen warriors leapt towards them, each armed with laser swords, which flashed against the Sikari's as they battled, an acrobatic explosion of power and destruction until the female warriors' blades sliced through their opposition, and they lay dead at their feet.

A few moments later, the Sikari stood at the clear plexiglass door.

A few seconds later, Tanara was behind it.

And she had what she had come to take.

A long, rectangular, black and gold box, covered with silver sigils.

Containing an ancient relic.

One which the Thule and the other secret societies had all first thought invaluable.

But which they now, mistakenly, thought worthless.

Which only the Sikari knew was far from worthless.

Instead, it was an ancient secret only they knew how to unlock.

Which they had come to claim.

To reclaim.

Once more as their own.

The shroud.

The shroud of Turin.

To be continued in

Book Two Of

The DisIntegration Trilogy . . .


A.k.a.

Book Four Of

The Arimathean Saga...

THE ARIMATHEAN SAGA

BOOK ONE:  THE ARIMATHEAN

BOOK TWO:  THE BLOOD OF DESTINY

BOOK THREE:  BLACK KNIGHT APOCALYPSE

BOOK FOUR: T.B.A.

BOOK FIVE: DISINTEGRATION

# Other Books By Sean Leary

**The Arimathean** (novel)

**The Blood of Destiny** (novel)

**Black Knight Apocalypse** (novel)

**Does The Shed Skin Know It Was Once A Snake?**
(short stories)

**Every Number Is Lucky To Someone**

(short stories)

**My Life As A Freak Magnet**

(short stories)

**Exorcising Ghosts**

(graphic novel)

**Here Comes The Goot!**

(children's/beginning readers)

**Go, Racecars, Go!**

(children's/beginning readers)

**Nine Little Penguin Ninjas**

(children's/beginning readers)

**Baby Bird**

(children's/beginning readers)

**We Are All Characters**

(children's/beginning readers)

**Beautiful Remnants of Chaotic Failures**

(poetry)

**Danger Maps**

(poetry)

**Every Broken Heart Creates The Pieces That Will Pave The Way To The Place Your Heart Will Call Home**

(poetry)

**Tricks of the Light**

(poetry)

**The Soft Venom of Promise**

(poetry)

**The Night Universal**

(poetry)

**There Is Truth In The Untamed Beat of a Heart**

(poetry)

**We Are Shadows In The Absence of Light**

(poetry)

**Sean Leary's Greatest Hits, volume one**

(humor)

**Sean Leary's Greatest Hits, volume two**

(humor)

**Your Favorite Band**

(stageplay / screenplay)

**Dingo Boogaloo**

(stageplay / screenplay)

**Rock City Live!**

(stageplay / screenplay)

**My Life As A Freak Magnet: The Scripts**

(stageplay / screenplay)

**Shots To The Heart**

(stageplay)

**This Is The Best Worst Idea I Ever Had**

(short stories)

**The I Can't Even Adult Coloring Book**

(coloring book)

For more writing and more information, see
www.seanleary.com and www.thearimathean.com.

www.ingramcontent.com/pod-product-compliance
Lightning Source LLC
Chambersburg PA
CBHW030345020726
47493CB00003B/685